ANTOLIN

ANTOLIN

THE MAN AND THE SHADOW

Evelyn Regner Seno

To order additional copies of this book, contact:
Xlibris
1-800-455-039
www.Xlibris.com.au
Orders@Xlibris.com.au
758088

TABLE OF CONTENTS

Important Note vii
Preface ix
Prologue xiii
La Vida Del Campo xv
Himno xix

DISCUSSION I - Early Search 1

    Chapter 1: Twilight in Talisay 7
    Chapter 2: The Inner Volcano 15
    Chapter 3: Nicolasa 21

DISCUSSION II - The Scholar 29

    Chapter 4: The Revelation 45
    Chapter 5: Haciendas de Talisay 51
    Chapter 6: The Encomendero 57

DISCUSSION III - The Grand Rebellion 61

    Chapter 7: Eustaquia 69
    Chapter 8: Paradise Lost 73
    Chapter 9: The Miracle 81
    Chapter 10: The Catharsis 85
    Chapter 11: Utter Devotion 89
    Chapter 12: The Second Child 92
    Chapter 13: Apolonio, The Heroic Layman 98

DISCUSSION IV - The Women 103

    Chapter 14: Sunrise in Naga.. 117

    Chapter 15: The Suarez Family...123

    Chapter 16: Aleja..130

    Chapter 17: Darkness and Light 134

    Chapter 18: The Resolute Woman 137

    Chapter 19: Minglanilla, The Brewing Cauldron....................140

    Chapter 20: Fidelina 148

DISCUSSION V - The Search Continues...............................153

    Chapter 21: Unleashed Fury.. 157

    Chapter 22: Argao, The Last Stop..................................... 161

DISCUSSION VI - The Advocate...171

    Chapter 23: The Happy Family 193

    Chapter 24: Renewed Hope - The American Regime.............197

    Chapter 25: Paradise Regained 202

    Chapter 26: Fausto 209

DISCUSSION VII - The Reunion 211

    Chapter 27: The Truth Sets Me Free................................. 217

DISCUSSION VIII - 221

Published Works Of Fr. Antolin Frias y Ramos, OSA 223

The Descendants Of Antolin Frias y Ramos 225

References 229

The Author Speaks 231

IMPORTANT NOTE

In this book, **the life of Fr. Antolin Frias, OSA** is set against the backdrop of the **late nineteenth century Philippines**. How do both individual and society cope in this crucial period in Philippine history?

Where is the truth? The truth is revealed in many ways.

It comes through **hard data presented in records and documents**. It is also revealed through **prevailing, powerful folklore** passed on through the generations by reliable witnesses.

And the truth is also revealed to us **through our feelings**. After weighing the hard facts and folklore, one's intuition is stirred to dig deeper into the story. Endless possibilities can emerge from what has been revealed on the surface.

This book, therefore, is a unique blend of **a HISTORICAL NOVEL AND DISCUSSIONS WITH DOCUMENTARY**.

The **DISCUSSIONS** provide the historical data – actual people, facts, and prevailing folklore – with views and reflections thrown in. References have been mentioned in the dialogue and in the References Section at the end of the book. These have been supported by photographs.

The **NOVEL**, on the other hand, is a work of fiction, purely speculative but closely based on the facts and folklore mentioned in the Discussions.

The actual characters' names have been retained in a purely fictional novel. Knowing this, the readers have a choice to suspend their disbelief and dwell on probabilities, to use their imagination to wonder what could have happened instead of simply believing what limited facts have been revealed in the Discussions.

Typical figures of the times – the encomendero, the tenant, the natives, the illustrado, the women, the mother, the rebels, the Spanish friar, and others – have all been represented by fictional characters. Creating them has been a result of so much research plus intuition and imagination.

A work of fiction could best enhance the truth with magic, poetry, and romance. What other genre would best add flesh and color to life stories? **How else portray the moral struggle?**

Some **photographs** have been cited for source. Photographs without citations belong to the author.

Footnotes are found at the end of each chapter.

EVELYN REGNER SENO

PREFACE

"Hija!"

One word echoes through time and space.

"Hija", a half-Spanish grandfather calls. I come running. He holds my little face between his gnarled hands and looks deep into my eyes.

I am six years old, at the mercy of this beloved old man. And each time he lets me go, I am transformed.

"Hija!"

Another voice calls.

But this time I am imagining it. The voice belongs to my great grandfather, **Antolin Frias y Ramos**. I never met him, though his portrait has hung on my wall for many years. He is reaching out to us, his descendants, calling out from the past century - seeking to be known, understood, and honored. His message is more felt than heard.

And I am at his feet. He would have been one to call out *'hija'* – "child" - an entire world in a word – that age of innocence and wonder - when the wrath of a punishing god was believed to bring thunder, lightning, and rain.

Having been born in 1947, I witnessed the transition from this age of magic and mystery into the age of certainty, when science and technology threatened all illusions. But as we all grow older and a bit jaded, we find we miss that little dose of magic.

Thus the incredible drive to write this book on Antolin Frias. To write about him would be to portray an age when one gaped at a rainbow. His life portrays how innocence and ignorance most often led

ix

to heartache, and how both individual and nation rose from the ashes and triumphed.

To instill love and honor for a man, a people, and a nation is the main aim of this book.

So, what really happened in the life of **ANTOLIN FRIAS Y RAMOS?**

Beyond any fact and folklore, one's heart and intuition can be stirred to dig deeper into the heart and soul of a beloved subject. So I have tried to portray Father Frias as sublime and noble, though with feet made of clay.

My search for my great grandfather has required no less than a total commitment. Of a life lived more than a century ago, just how much data can one gather? Church and municipal records in Cebu were destroyed during the last world war. Old pictures and memorabilia have been lost. Graves in old cemeteries have disappeared. People who knew the story have died or lost their recall.

Fortunately, Padre Frias played an important role in the history of Cebu. The **Order of Saint Augustine** has faithfully kept records of all their members, found at the **San Agustin Church in Intramuros, Manila, at the Basilica del Santo Nino in Cebu, and at the Real Colegio Seminario de los Padres Agustinos Filipinos in Valladolid, Spain.**

The limited information that was passed on about our great grandfather, the Spanish friar, would not have done him justice. The mere mention of his name has always been followed by a question, like: **"Wasn't he the 'frayle' who had children by several women? Just look at our light brown eyes – or is it green?"** So he, by some accident of nature, was simply the one who gave us all our light-brown-almost-green eyes. Sad that such a brave and talented man like him would be reduced to this single impression among his descendants.

But cousin **Dr. Romeo Regner-Du**, who initiated the interest on Father Frias, changed all that for us. He distributed pictures of Father Frias among the relatives, and told us that our great-grandfather was

a writer and an intellectual. That struck a sensitive chord in me. I resolved to search him extensively and write about him.

Many years passed and I had not written a word. Then, one day, my sister, **Joy Regner,** acted on an inspiration and walked the **Camino de Santiago** pilgrimage in Spain. This Road would take her through the city of Burgos, around which Father Frias was born and bred and educated at the nearby **Real Seminario de los Padres Agustinos Filipinos in Valladolid**. The trip finally sealed my resolve to write a book on our great grandfather, the priest.

The rapidly changing times in the late nineteenth century Philippines, with the brewing rebellion against the Spaniards - especially the wealthy and powerful friar orders -presented numerous challenges to Fr. Frias. But apparently the same spirit, which it took the young man to become a priest and embark on an arduous journey to this far-flung colony, enabled him to emerge wounded but victorious.

EVELYN REGNER SENO – Author

PROLOGUE

This story starts in the year 1881 in Cebu, a province of the Spanish colony, Las Islas Filipinas.

Three centuries have passed since the Spaniards established the colony Las Islas Filipinas and Christianized it through the Sword and the Cross. The Spanish friar orders – Augustinians, Recollects, Dominicans, Franciscans, Jesuits – subdivided the missionary work among themselves. Aside from pastoral work, the friars performed numerous roles. They elevated the natives to a higher culture and civilization by introducing art and science; helped the civil government by acting as advocates, law enforcers, builders; protected the natives against the abuses of the encomenderos (large landowners); ran the poorly funded schools; organized community affairs, and numerous other tasks. They were first to go to the remotest places, paving the way for the civil officials. The friar orders also owned large tracts of land around the colony which native tenants leased and cultivated.

Due to the frequent turnover of civil officials (a result of the chaotic political state in Spain), the more stable friars became the bulwark of Philippine society, acquiring much power and influence. Travelers to the colony - officials, scholars, tradesmen, etc. – attested to the respect, reverence and gratitude with which the natives regarded the friars.

However, the 1880's witnessed a change in the natives' attitude toward the friars. Propaganda accused them generally of abusive behavior, excessive economic interests and political authority. Though some of the friars were undoubtedly guilty of these accusations, historians have claimed that these were the minority. Furthermore, these priests already working under severely stressful conditions, were isolated in large, remote areas. Though the cases of misconduct were isolated, they glared against the natives' high expectations of the revered group.

Then the large friar lands became a central issue. These lands were acquired in time through donations from the government and private individuals. In reality, the friar orders did not profit much from the lease or produce of the lands, after improvements and other expenses were met. The native tenants had everything to gain in these cases.

But the insurrection of 1896 demanded the expulsion of the friars. The rebels clamored for the Spanish friars to relinquish their roles and their parishes to the native clergy. The friars gradually turned into pariahs – many were imprisoned, tortured, and executed by the rebels towards the Revolution of 1898. Many of them went into hiding or fled out of the country.

Much of the Philosophy of the Enlightenment, an expanded idea of freedom, which had influenced the French Revolution (1789) and other revolutions around the globe, also touched the Philippine colony through the minds of a new class of educated natives called "illustrados". The "illustrados" demanded changes through peaceful means but did not succeed in controlling the violence and the bloodshed that brought about these changes.

LA VIDA DEL CAMPO

(Imitacion de Pope)

Feliz el hombre que afanoso labra
De tierno padre la preciada herencia,
Y alegre aspira del nativo suelo
El puro ambiente.

Libre del yugo de ambición mezquina,
De envidia ageno y de salud colmado,
Halla en el campo de inocencia asilo,
Paz y ventura.

Alli, tendido en la vecina loma,
Ve sus rebaños en la selva umbria;
La mansa oveja y las ligeras cabras,
Ricas de leche.

Tiende su vista á la feraz llanura,
Y vé que á impulso dela brisa ondean,
Las ricas mieses de dorada espiga,
En mansas ondas.

En verde soto y en pensil ameno
Pasa las horas del ardiente estio;
Y atento escucha de canoras aves
Las melodias.

¡Alma sencilla que al nacer la aurora
Eleva al cielo su filial plegaria!

Nunca importunos ni el dolor ni llanto
Su dicha turben.
Feliz el hombre que del patrio suelo
El aire puro y aromoso aspira!
Campos alegres que ofreceis al alma
Paz y ventura!

Aqui, á la sombra, en el florido césped,
Y á las orillas de argentado rio,
Viva yo alegre sin oir los ecos
Vanos del mundo.

Aqui dormido en silenciosa tumba
En paz repose, sin mundana pompa,
Ni en oro y mármol, ni aun en leve polvo
Graben mi nombre.

Flores tan solo de sencillo caliz
Brote la tierra, y al viajero digan
Que alli algun dia nacera mas bella
Una flor virgen.

De paz el Angel mi sepulcro vele,
Y al fiel amigo que vera en mi tumba,
Mira, le diga, señalando al cielo
Esa es su patria.

Fr. Antolin Frias y Ramos, La Vid y Agosto de 1881

REVISTAS AUGUSTINIANA, 1986, pp.286-287

LA VIDA DEL CAMPO

(A Translation)

COUNTRY LIFE
(In Imitation of Pope)

Happy man eager for life
Tender father of the precious heritage,
And cheerful sucking native soil
A pure environment.

Free from the yoke of petty ambition,
Of envy and greed,
Here in the field of sacred innocence,
Peace and bliss.

There, lying on the neighboring hill,
Go their flocks in the shady forest;
The meek sheep and goats light,
Rich milk.

It tends to view its fertile plains,
And feel the breeze's pulse flutter,
Among the rich harvests of golden spike,
In gentle waves.

Fields of green and pleasant vines,
Bask in the burning sun;
While the songbirds listen and sing,
Their melodies.

Simple soul on whom,
At birth the aurora shone,
His prayer rises to subsidiary heaven!
Never obtrusive nor crying nor pain.
Happy man of his homeland,
The pure air and aromas suck!
In camps he offers his soul,
Peace and bliss!

Here, in the shade, in the flowery grass,
And on the banks of silvery river,
I live cheerful without hearing the echoes,
The Vain world.

Here asleep in silent grave
Rest in peace, without worldly pomp,
Neither gold and marble, nor even light powder,
My name engraved.

Flowers of simple calyx
Buds of earth tell the passers,
That someday there will be born more beautiful,
A virgin flower.

An Angel of Peace protects my grave,
Where the faithful friend stands,
Look, it says, pointing to heaven,
That is your homeland.

(Fr. Antolin Frias y Ramos)

Translated by the Author

HIMNO

Gloria, Gloria al ilustre Prelado
De esta Iglesia preclaro Pastor:
De virtudes y ciencia dechado,
Mensajero de paz y de amor.

Estrofa 1.

Veis del Cielo el Astro fulgente
Declinar trias la cumber del monte…?
Negra noche cubrió el horizonte,
Y la tierra envolvió en su capùz.

Más…volved vuestros ojos á Oriente,
Y vereis sonreir nueva aurora…
Y las cumbres el nuevo sol dora
Esparciendo torrentes de luz.

Coro. Gloria, Gloria etc.

Estrofa 2.

Asi un dia, de luto vestida
Por su Obispo la Iglesia cebuana
Vislumbraba una aurora lejana,
Que debia ahuyentar su dolor.
Y al brillar hoy la luz bendecida,
Y, borrando del llanto la huella,
Te saluda cual fulgida estrella
Mensajera de paz y de amor.
Coro, Gloria, gloria etc.

Estrofa 3.

!Bienvenido, amoroso Prelado!
á un pedazo de tierra española,
Donde el lábaro Santo tremola,
Y de España el glorioso Pendón.
!Quiera el Cielo que un dia á tu lado,
   Lejos, lejos del misero suelo,
En la cumbre gloriosa del Cielo,
   Adoremos al Dios de Sion!

Coro.

Gloria, Gloria al Ilustre prelado,
De esta Iglesia preclaro Pastor:
De virtudes y ciencia dechado,
   Mensajero de paz y de amor.

FR. ANTOLIN FRIAS
Agustino
San Nicolas 4 de Enero de 1887

Cronica Agustiniana, 1887, p.368

HYMN

English Translation

Glory, Glory to the illustrious prelate
In this church an illustrious Pastor :
Paragon of virtue and science,
Messenger of peace and love.

Verse 1

See the heavens of stars glittering
Decline behind the mountains ...?
Black night covers the horizon,
And the earth envelops in his hood.

Then ... turn your eyes to the East,
And you will see the new dawn smile ...
And the new sun peaks dora
Torrents of light scattering.
Coro. Gloria, Gloria etc.

Verse 2

So one day, dressed in mourning
For his Bishop's Cebuano Church
Glimpsed a distant dawn,
That ought to scare her pain.
And now the blessed light shine,
And, erasing the traces of tears,
Which greets eastern star
Messenger of peace and love.
Coro, Glory, glory etc.

Verse 3

! Welcome, loving bishop !
To a Spanish piece of land,
Where sacred work vibrates

And the glorious Spanish flag.
! May Heaven one day by your side,
Far, far from miserable soil,
In the glorious summit of Heaven,
Worship the God of Zion !

Chorus

Gloria, Gloria the illustrious prelate,
In this church an illustrious Pastor :
Paragon of virtue and science,
Messenger of peace and love.

San Nicolas January 4, 1887

Fr. Antolin Frias, OSA

Translated by the Author

FATHER ANTOLIN FRIAS Y RAMOS, OSA
(1857 - 1925)

PHOTO COURTESY OF DR. ROMEO REGNER DU

AND THE TRUTH SHALL SET YOU FREE

(John 8:32)

Crossroads in our life's journey can present us with a huge challenge. The road we choose would make all the difference. One direction could lead to disaster, the other to redemption. Where is the answer? Opposing forces within us and around us lead us to review our lives. A resolution must be made to find the Truth. The Truth ultimately leads to Freedom.

But what is Truth? According to the German philosopher, Wilhelm Friedrich Hegel, the truth is a manifestation of God's Will. The challenge lies in finding truth in the maze of untruths.

In our story, the world is fast evolving around the master and the slave. Ideas of democracy are slowly seeping into the Spanish colony, Las Islas Filipinas, now endangered by impending mass rebellion, shaken from its roots.

Our central character, a Spanish friar, finds himself threatened by this unstable social environment. As an individual, he also has his own Inner Conflicts. The Turmoil has planted Seeds of Doubt in his heart. He has made sacred vows and promises to God, King, and Self. This is his Master. But his loyalties have been shaken by the forces around him. He yearns only for the truth. He knows the Truth will set him free.

And so begins his moral struggle.

(Inspired by the philosophy of Wilhelm Friedrich Hegel)

DISCUSSION I
Early Search

"*Unbelievable,*" *I whispered, as we gazed transfixed at centuries-old church vestments,* "*all that needlework! So intricate, so delicate, with metallic thread still glowing after so many centuries!*"

My cousin E., an old friend M., and I were in the **San Miguel Parish Museum in Argao**, *a large township 60 kms south of Cebu City.*

"*The women must have done it, with just a candle or two…*"

"*Or a single gas lamp*".

"*As only a native woman would… for the white man…the priest… ruining her eyes…breaking her back…a half-blind, bent old woman in the end.*"

"*You seem to know exactly how it feels to be her.*"

"*To have loved him so much, to be willing to go blind, to break her back, to bear a child. And, in the end, to be abandoned…*"

"*You are talking about* **Lola Asay**, *or* **Nicolasa Bascon**, *aren't you? Yes, common belief has it that she and her sister* **Eustaquia** *or Yayang worked around the church convento, like so many native women, doing intricate vestments. They also sang in the choir. This happened in Talisay*".

"*But she certainly did not go blind. After she had a child, she seemed to have moved on. To say she was 'abandoned' would be rash. Nobody knows the exact story.*"

"*My instincts tell me she never even told him and ran away instead - a woman ahead of her time. I can safely assume this knowing how the women in this side of our family have always been strong and self-sufficient.*"

"*Is she the one who bore a child by that priest?*"

"*Please don't call him 'that priest'. He had a name. It's* **Antolin Frias**," I said, rolling his name with my tongue like a regular Spaniard, savoring the magic of each sound.

"*You sound like you're really proud of him. And so this Lola Asay did all the lovely attire? Her ultimate reward - the sight of him wearing them, looking absolutely divine!*"

"*And he would have changed shape and color so swiftly as soon as he left the altar, just like a chameleon? Is that what you're thinking?*"

"*As anyone is bound to think of such liaisons.*"

"*I happen to be the product of just such a liaison. Do you think I and my family are any less sacred?*"

Ms. Class valedictorian was caught speechless.

We continued to browse in the museum in this centuries-old town with its well-preserved church compound and museum dating back to the seventeenth century Spanish colonial period.

"*But how are you so sure the priest was your great ancestor?*"

"*Some folklore only becomes richer and more credible through the ages. This one has even become more convincing…*"

"*How so? Have you found some DNA at last? Maybe some were lurking in these vestments and chalices?*"

"*This is not some crime movie.*"

A pregnant silence descended on us as we tried to absorb the spirit of the past. "*Look, there happens to be a very dominant family trait, and it could only come from him and nobody else.*" I broke into our reverie.

"*And that would be…*"

"*Eyes flecked light brown and green. I believe that's called 'hazel'. Our grandmother,* **Fidelina or Lola Peding**, *the priest's daughter, had them. People would stare at her and remark: 'anak gyud ka sa Frayle, o', (you are really the friar's daughter).*"

"*And she would give a smile full of meaning.*"

2

"*A smile which meant she was glad to be 'recognized'. He was her father.*"

"*She must have kept a safe distance from her father as she grew up, and needed other people to tell her she was his daughter*".

"*So, these **hazel eyes** are like a trademark,*" *I said with a trace of humor, "Just to let you know the product is genuine.*"

"*Oh yes – such power!*" *E. answered, excited at the idea, "They've worked wonders for us. They're great for expressing joy, sadness, anger, empathy, compassion, and, of course, I should not forget – love*".

The sound of someone's voice saying, "I love your eyes", echoed in my mind. That sealed our fate together - his and mine.

"*For sure, I have been passionately loved for nothing else but these eyes. I also have been just as strongly hated for them, 'cuz they're great for staring people in place.*"

"*Hazel eyes are a recessive gene which persists through generations. The degree of lightness varies between individuals… some have it greener than brown and others vice-versa. The color changes with the light, the mood, and even the make-up. Just like a chameleon.*"

"*They certainly get things done without so many words said*" *I added.*

"*Oh, yes, I only have to give Danny that look and he melts away like butter,*" *E. joked, referring to her teenage boy.*

*With some awe, I realized that the hazel eyes passed itself on to my children - now the fifth generation from **Father Antolin**.*

"*Wow, it's like that priest - I'm sorry, Fr. Frias - left some kind of trademark on his descendants,*" *M. finally understood.*

"*Or, it could be God…He always puts everything in place, doesn't He?*" *I said, bells ringing in my mind. "We don't need that great philosopher to tell us that the whole world is God's Will and Idea.*"

*I was searching my mind for a name when M., the class wizard, said, "Maybe those hazel eyes are some kind of synthesis. You remember our Philosophy class …**Hegel**…a synthesis resulting from a struggle between opposing forces?*"

"*Opposing forces is correct. How could I forget dear old Hegel? And that charming nutty professor, Brother Arnold? A struggle for the Truth to set us free, etc. etc. Our ancestors in those changing times – the nineteenth*

3

century – torn apart by opposing forces – personal and political – class struggle – racial conflict – their world upside down – you're the whiz, M."

Hazel eyes – a synthesis - God's Will and Idea, His signature.

"Now, I wonder, maybe I should look into my revered ancestor and write a book about him…To honor his memory – finally – and put a stop to that snickering on top of his grave. No one deserves to be blamed for many a family karma," I suggested.

"How will you manage to write a book with such limited data available?" asked M.

"There are just enough facts and folklore around which to build a sound story. I was told by a History expert that folklore can be just as reliable as plain facts. Now, I would like to put myself in the mind of **Father Antolin Frias y Ramos,"** *I resolved.*

"But, perhaps I should write a work of fiction. For me, imaginative literature would best portray the inner struggle. It can best arouse the imagination by presenting everything in a more human light," I added, "but of course just like in any historical novel the facts and the folklore must be based on actual data."

"Will the real names of the characters be retained in the novel?" M. asked.

"Yes, I think that would be more effective. After all, the reader will be informed that the story itself is a fictional interpretation of actual facts," I replied.

"So where exactly was Fr. Frias assigned here in Cebu?"

"At the San Agustin Church in Intramuros, Manila, I was shown the **MISION CV DE RELIGIOSOS,** *a directory of all the religious who had served in the Order of St. Augustine," I told everyone, reaching for my notes. "Now, this is where he was all those years he spent in Cebu."*

I read out from my notes while everyone listened in rapt attention.

"Father Antolin Frias served as parish priest of several parishes in Cebu province, which was then known as **LA PROVINCIA DE SANTISSIMO NOMBRE DE JESUS."**

"From **1881 to 1887,** *Frias served as parish priest of the* **Parish of Sta. Teresa de Avila in Talisay.** *Simultaneously, he served in the* **Parish**

4

of San Nicolas right in the Ciudad. *Note, he would have been only in his early twenties then."*

"A puppy thrown to the wolves," someone exclaimed.

"Yes," I replied, "the wolves here being natives already angered at the conditions of many centuries of Spanish domination. Anyway, from **1889 to 1890**, *he served as parish priest of the Parish of* **Naga**. *From* **1891 to 1895** *he served as parish priest of the Parish of* **Minglanilla**.

"Finally, Fr. Frias was assigned in the Parish of **Argao** *from* **1897 to 1898**. *This assignment was prematurely terminated when Frias disappeared to spare himself from the* **Katipuneros'** *wrath.*

"In addition to his parish duties," cousin Susan volunteered, "Fr. Frias also appears on record as the **Administrador de Haciendas de Talisay.**

"I know," I said, "and this was a mean feat. The haciendas *covered an area of* **8,100 hectares**. *The entire towns of Talisay and Minglanilla from the seashore to the distant hills, these friar lands were cultivated with coconuts, rice, corn, nipa, and sugar in addition to the livestock. They were all rented out to native tenants".*

"So, how could he have travelled around such a large area in the absence of roads?" someone asked.

"I've thought about that. We can safely presume that he travelled most conveniently only on horseback. And we imagine that he would have been an expert horseman from his youth. Remember the wide hills and valleys around Castrogeriz? He would have guided his horse efficiently through the banks of the river between the low hills of Talisay and Minglanilla," I told them.

"But this was the least of his problems. The tenants in the nineteenth century colony hardly paid their rentals. They were frequently at odds with the neighboring Spanish hacienderos.

"The friar orders and the colony as a whole were losing money from agricultural venture Fr. Frias would have had to deal with all these problems." "And significantly he was also the one in-charge of the **Archiveros de Provincia de Cebu.**

"The entire archives of the province?" someone asked, incredulous.

"What better person to do the task than one who was known to be a scholar and an intellectual?" I finally ended my little lecture.

CHAPTER 1

TWILIGHT IN TALISAY

One day my life took a turning point. It was the day my life really began. Before that day, I was just living in my dreams.

Strange how, for many years, my dream life had seemed more real than my waking life – until that day. With each day, I could hardly wait for night to descend and bring me a different world in my sleep. In my dreams, I laughed, I wept, I loved, I was loved – it was a world where I was more human, more alive.

Until one late afternoon in May in the year 1883. Very warm, like any summer day in Talisay. I was taking my usual late afternoon stroll – a time I always set aside for quiet contemplation as the sun set behind the distant hills. For just a few precious minutes, the sky, the sea, and the sand would all turn a brilliant orange. And for a while there, I would bask in the surrounding magic and forget the sweltering heat, the suffocating humidity, and the mosquitoes. The mosquitoes, especially, which brought the fever I was terrified would kill me one day. But it made life easier to bear to offer all for the forgiveness of sins - an idea long pounded in me – or so they said.

They made it sound so simple. To be honest, I felt like I was drowning. The truth is, as twilight set in, a deep sadness would descend on me. And I had to get out there and become one with the wide open sky. That melancholy, that profound nostalgia…it was driving me mad.

They made it sound so easy.

The Parish of Sta. Teresa de Avila
Talisay, Cebu

Talisay was a village way back in the pre-Spanish era, then became an estate of the Augustinians in early 1648. Just like the other towns in the south of the Ciudad de Cebu (Cebu City), it was once just a "visita" or chapel of the San Nicolas parish. The town itself was organized in 1849. The name 'talisay" was derived from the "Magtalisay" tree, found in abundance around the town. Another more essential resource in the town is the abundant water lying just below the ground level. It is also famous for its beaches, which attracted visitors from the Ciudad through the centuries until urbanization took over in recent years.

Talisay was separated from San Nicolas in 1834 and became a parish on its own with the patron saint Sta. Teresa de Jesus de Avila. The parish priest, Fr. Antolin Frias, OSA, appears on record as one who assisted the capitan in organizing the government.

Talisay is the hometown of the brothers known as the "Tres Alinos" (the three Alinos) who took active part in the revolution against Spain.

Talisay was converted into a city on Jan. 12, 2001, a metropolitan spread of the City of Cebu.

At other times of the day, I was too busy to be lonely. In Talisay, just a few miles from the larger Ciudad de Cebu, I had been the only Spaniard for miles around. I was supposed to be lonely – the young and warm-blooded creature that I was. But what energy, what spirit was there left to feel lonely? I was drained of my very spirit. There was just too much work and too little time that at the end of each hectic day, I would doze off the minute my head touched my pillow.

And then I would be soaked with dreams.

But these twilight hours – they transformed me. Then, I could feel. I became human.

I had always been told, while growing up, that I was strong - resilient – like the wheat bending with the wind. Growing up in the middle of wheat fields stretching into the horizon, I learned to live inside myself, in an inner world shaped according to my whims. This was how one survived the same infinite isolation in this little town of Talisay.

Two years had passed since 1881, when I came off that steamboat from Spain – a six-week-long journey I would never forget. My nausea was so severe I lost all my bearings and floated in midair between the floor and the ceiling. I could not swallow more than a morsel at a time until the ship docked in Manila. Why, I believe I simply stumbled off it, emaciated and half dead.

This story should be something a grandfather would be proud to tell his grandchildren. But wait, how could I even think of grandchildren when I would never get married? I always give a little chuckle at the thought of it. I had taken those *¹vows*, yes, those sacred promises, with my body prostrate on the floor in front of the altar. I vowed never to love a woman the way ordinary men do, never to get married, never to beget children…how could I have been so sure of myself at the age of nineteen?

Finally, here in Talisay, since I took over as parish priest two years ago, I had dared to take off my habit and dress like any man to fit the situation. That Augustinian habit was mortifying! As though the long sleeves were not enough, there had to be a large cowl.

And on that day in that beach, I was wearing only a white pair of collarless cotton knit shirt and loose muslin pants folded up to my knees.

Just like a fisherman – though I no doubt smelled a lot better. I savored the feel of the wet brown sand on my bare feet. I laughed at the way the people stared at me when I dressed down. Was it the hair on my arms and legs?

But everyone should have long realized that I was a mere mortal just like everyone else. I heaved a deep sigh of sadness. All the shameful things I dreamed about in my sleep – if only they knew! Then they would be astonished to find that I was, after all, just flesh, blood, and bones - just another warm blooded creature, at the mercy of my pain and my pleasure and my all too human needs.

Like, right then, oh, I was so hungry for a friend – not any of those rich matrons and spinsters who gazed up at me, starry-eyed, from below the pulpit. Not any of those shifty-eyed farmers in the haciendas. Not just a friend, but more like a mother.

"Padre, padre!" singsong voices called out to me. Those were the usual children, priest-watchers sitting here each day waiting for me to pass by. I dug into my pocket for some homemade sweets and gave each one an equal share. "Say '*gracias*'," I coached them to say thanks. Instead, they just laughed and ran away happy. Then, I saw the usual teenage girls ogling at me from under a Magtalisay tree. All four started to giggle as I passed. I waved at them, said a cheerful 'Ola!' with a big smile. They all blushed and giggled louder.

"I didn't hear that," I teased them. "Say '*ola, padre*'"

"Ooola, padri," one of them blurted out. Peals of young laughter pierced the air.

[2]"*Buenas Tardes.* [3]*Maayong hapon.*" I shouted out at two fishermen on the shore, using every chance to teach Spanish. They smiled and waved.

As the birds were settling for the night in the huge Magtalisay trees, I basked in the cacophony – the raucous of waves and birds and crickets – just what I needed at the end of days spent riding my horse under the punishing sun, through a maddening monotony of endless corn and sugar cane fields.

In *Castrogeriz*, the town in northern Spain where I grew up, there was only a little river. We children could bathe in it only in the summer, when the weather turned warm. But my parents would take me and my siblings to the Atlantic coast once a year before the autumn came. We would take a carriage to the coast in San Sebastian, then cross the hills of this Basque region into France, and head to the famous beach resorts of Biarritz.

These were the times when I would see my mother at her happiest, her smile brimming under the wide straw hat. The breezes from the Atlantic Ocean were believed to be curative, and my mother had always been frail. She had lost several pregnancies

⁴"Mama...*donde estas?*" I whispered to the trees, my heart filled with an old longing.

But all this had to stop when I was ten years old. We stopped going anywhere after the event – that terrible loss - I pushed the thought away as swiftly as it occurred.

No, no, one day at a time, I would simply whisper.

Here in Talisay I could smell the sea and the surrounding mangrove swamps from the convento. The sound of the waves would lull me to sleep. I kept dreaming of a day when I could sneak into the water for a swim, but this I would have to do in the dark, at night when nobody was looking. With all this water, my life was not completely impoverished.

The dream to serve my fellowmen in a sublime way was cultivated in me as a boy. Yet how I ended up within the strict confines of a seminary at the age of seventeen was a memory I pushed back as quickly as it came. As though I really had much choice under those circumstances...

"Becoming a priest is the noblest thing to do for a bright, young man like you," Papa would tell me every evening at dinner, "think of how many heathen souls you will save by going to the colonies."

I tried to turn a deaf ear to his little speech as I gobbled up my pastries for dessert. My professors spoke of me as a serious and introspective student with a talent for writing and speaking. After hearing this, Papa could not rest until I had achieved his dream for me.

Everyone's best intentions to serve God and King drove me to do service here. But the burden had been tremendous. The position of both religious and civic leader came with high expectations. We friars took pains to learn the native dialect, Binisaya, because the natives were not willing to learn Spanish. For years, I had fallen asleep each night still holding the language book, "Arte de la Lengua Cebuana", in my hand.

Then, we friars had to teach reading, writing, religion, arithmetic, and crafts in makeshift classrooms in a perpetual state of disrepair. The supervision of the building of roads and infrastructure fell into our hands. We took charge of the large church landholdings, while numerous parish duties, like early morning mass, novenas, and the sacraments already put our stamina to a severe test. We had been priest, teacher, civic leader, advocate, and even guardia civil, settling disputes in the absence of authorities.

And even then, young as I was, I had been given these large friar *haciendas* to manage. And just because they knew that I was such a good horseman. There was 8000 hectares of it to inspect, after all. How else to go around but on the back of dear, old Pepito, my stallion?

All we expected in return from the natives was absolute loyalty and support. It was good in the beginning. But soon after I settled in, I immediately sensed an air of resentment and hostility around these [5] *indios*.

The natives smiled just a bit too much. They pretended to obey my every wish. But I have had the soul of a poet, a sensitive man, and I keenly felt the seething rancor, the ridicule just below the surface. The other friars around the colony suffered the same treatment. The very air crackled with anger and resentment. This was especially felt in the 1800's.

It was the times, the 19th century after the French Revolution. Liberty! Fraternity! Equality! The "slave" and the "master" must then learn to co-exist in a wholesome interdependence. But such changes always meant bloodshed. All this philosophy about the dignity of man and the meaning of freedom would slowly seep into this far-flung colony and end up in a final rebellion. I always felt giddy at the thought of violence.

Just the day before, my native servant Nardo broke one of my favorite china. It was a precious century-old porcelain, a family heirloom which I took pains to carry all the way from Spain. With alarming regularity, Gracia, Nardo's wife, would burn my rice or lose my favorite socks or ruin my fragile cotton shirts. I would not have been surprised to find a frog in my bed one day soon.

Twilight in Talisay

Magtalisay trees around Talisay, Cebu

And just then, I heard the church bells toll the evening angelus. I remembered who I was and bowed my head to pray. [6]*"Ahora y en la hora de nuestro muerte, Amen."* Finishing the Hail Mary, I lifted up my face to a sky on fire. As the sun sank into the horizon, I closed my eyes to savor the cool evening breeze.

Then I heard a familiar sound – a woman weeping. Looking around, I saw long, dark hair through the thin trunk of a coconut tree. Stealthily creeping around the tree, I finally saw her sitting against it, hair covering her face. She looked up at me, startled.

"Hija?!" I exclaimed. "What happened? Are you hurt?"

The girl looked up startled, seemed to recognize me in an instant, then sprang up to her feet and sprinted away like a frightened rabbit. I watched her disappear into the *nipa* swamps. Then I realized that she was wearing the white cotton pants and shirt of a man.

---

[1] *the vows of celibacy*
[2] *Good afternoon, in Binisaya*
[3] *Good afternoon in Spanish*
[4] *Where are you? In Spanish*
[5] *The name used to classify the native Filipinos from the Spaniard*
[6] *Now and at the hour of our death, in Latin*

CHAPTER 2

THE INNER VOLCANO

That night sleep eluded me. I kept getting out of bed to look out the window at the moonlit garden below. I imagined I heard the cackle of chickens in the distance. But I seemed to be too moonstruck and strangely carefree to bother with the chickens.

A woman's distress, the sound of a heart breaking, and the sight of tears always stirred in me painful memories of that time – that time when I was just a boy, when the sound of crying women penetrated every nook of our large house.

But the most disturbing sound was the endless wailing of my newborn sister, Olimpia, crying out for Mama…

Only Papa was quiet – too quiet - my father's silence felt heavy for a long time. No, no…

I always pushed back the memories, way back into the innermost recesses of my mind.

I had seen the crying girl often before. I finally remembered that it was at a town fiesta in May the previous year. My heart quickened at the memory. She danced the courtship dance, the *cariñosa*. The coquettish figure in a beautiful gown, covering her face with a fan, flitted around in flirtatious movements with her partner – so much grace in that tall, lissome body.

It was a dance contest. She came out winner, and as she and her partner came off the little stage, on a wild impulse I got up from my seat and gave each of them a brotherly hug.

Then a shred of memory I had long suppressed threatened to emerge from one dark corner of my mind. Certainly now it was safe for me to dwell on it. Yes, in bed that night after the dance, with the sea breeze wafting from the wide open window, I finally allowed myself to recall the peculiar smell emanating from the lady dancer – what was it – a strange mix of coconut oil, and something else, something I could not name – the sea? So primeval – much as I imagined the aroma of the fluid in my mother's womb would smell.

And, oh yes, how could I have forgotten? That face had often been lifted up to me to receive the host in Holy Communion. Being human, I was struck by the pretty faces, the *ᵗmestizas* most of all. This girl had Malayan features, with a delicate button nose. The dark eyes were lit up with laughter. Not a face in any crowd. But she had this rare light complexion and height unusual for a native, and she carried herself erect with remarkable dignity. I had a strong sense of an inner strength emanating from her.

In the morning, feeling strangely refreshed in spite of a sleepless night, I hurried to the church to say the early morning mass. Coming home, as I settled at the table for my breakfast, I felt the palpable tension around my servants, Nardo and his wife, Gracia. Finally, the couple broke the news that all the chickens in the church backyard were gone. They must have run away, they said.

I could only give a helpless chuckle. The chickens ran away? For a moment, my mind strayed to a tale in my childhood, about a chicken who ran away, or was it a piglet? Then, I remembered the noise of chickens I had heard the previous night.

"No, Nardo, these chickens were stolen," I said as gently as I could, in my fluent Binisaya.

"Oh, no, Padre, nobody ever steals anything in this town," Gracia started to cry. "We natives are not a bunch of thieves as you Spaniards think!" she added, on the verge of hysteria.

Nardo simply looked down at his feet. "I'm very sorry, Padre, but there isn't even one chicken left for your table today," the wife added. "Should I just go to market, Padre?"

But this was a rare time when a woman's tears did not move me. They only served to annoy me. Without touching my bread and omelette, I stormed out of the house to find my horse. Wearing only cotton pants and shirt and black leather sandals, I rode off towards the surrounding fields. In the heat wave, riding fast, I must have looked like an angry apocalyptic horseman out to create havoc.

Chickens, chickens, this world was nothing but chickens – the words echoed in my head, in unison with the horse's gallop. It was not chickens. It was lies, lies, and more lies. The world was one huge lie, my life was one huge lie. It was all so pathetic!

My mind hazy with emotion, I had allowed my horse to break into a trot and travel in any direction. I had a vague sense of going through a sugar cane field. Finally, the horse stopped in front of a house which was blocking its way.

I came into a yard where a man was bent over caressing a rooster. Standing near him was a woman who seemed to be pounding away with a mortar and pestle.

"Ah, Padre!" the man exclaimed in surprise. [8]"*Maayong buntag. Asa man ka?*" he asked.

I remember alighting from my horse and standing before them, speechless and dazed from the heat, the sleeplessness, the empty stomach, and my fury.

"I lost my chickens…" I heard myself blurting out in Spanish.

"And did you come all this far to look for them?" asked the man in Binisaya, holding back his laughter. "Padre, you and I know your chickens would never get this far. But, please, please come up to the house. It's cool up there. [9]*Inday, palihug intawon*, go get some coconuts and make a nice, cool drink here for the Padre," he called out to the woman.

Without a word, I followed the man up to the house. I had known these people since I came to this parish. They were regular churchgoers - good, upright local folks, one of the oldest families of Talisay. For generations, this family had been one of the most trusted tenants in this part of the Friar haciendas, a barrio called *Dumlog*.

It was the family Bascon. I recognized the mother Bascon as a regular patron and donor of the parish.

The house was a wooden structure with a thatched roof. Its large living room had several doors leading to it from what could be bedrooms. But the man and I settled in comfortable bamboo chairs in a nice veranda overlooking an orchard and the sugar fields beyond. The man refrained from talking for quite a while. He was obviously the kind who respected the need for silence.

"Padre, I am sorry about your chickens. Do you think they were stolen?" the man finally asked, as we sipped our fresh coconut drinks. "Chickens are always in demand in May. It is the month of town fiestas."

The concern in his voice was unmistakable. I knew then that the friars were right to trust him and his ancestors all these years.

Then he enumerated the numerous fiesta celebrations in the surrounding barrios. Now I was increasingly convinced that my chickens were indeed stolen. But somehow it ceased to matter.

"There isn't even one left for my table today," I blurted out to the man, regretting it the next moment. I sounded like a whimpering child who had lost a favorite toy.

I knew something more violent than simply losing chickens had taken hold of my spirit.

"Oh, please, Padre, we can give you some chickens. We have so many of them. Clara here enjoys raising them. But Asay - you know my daughter, Nicolasa - would do such tasks grudgingly. No farmer – that one. Her heart is forever up in those clouds."

The man pretended to complain, but the love and the pride in his voice was unmistakable.

I feigned interest in the man's words. I was not really in any mood to hear a man talk about his children. But I felt myself relaxing in this house with this couple. For the first time since I came to this colony, I felt loved and totally at home.

The wife sat some distance away, watching me intently. Stealing glances at her I saw that her face wore that expression I often saw in some women – looking at me with hooded eyes and lips parted. What was her problem, I wondered, looking at me that way? I was sure she noticed that I was just of average height, like many Spaniards. And also that I was muscular and sturdy, like one who has worked close to the land. Not tall and patrician like one of the nobility. Really very ordinary...

"You have such a striking pair of eyes, and such strength in that lean body," the words always came with that same look, commenting on the the muscles burgeoning in my exposed arms – but that was before I became a priest.

Then, I felt Señora Bascon staring at my face, like she was taking in my aquiline nose, warmly sunburnt at the tip.

"You have such animal appeal. Yet, that wide forehead below a receding hairline suggests such powerful intelligence. And yet, you seem so vulnerable," I almost heard her saying, like the women before her.

I remember how those feminine guiles never ceased to amuse me, how I indulged them with the brightest of smiles and a word of thanks.

"When I look at you, a strange concoction of pleasure and dread creeps up in me," a servant girl once told me when I was just seventeen. We were pitching hay together and she obviously was trying to lure me into that inviting pile of hay.

But that same look from someone like Señora Bascon was a bit unsettling.

And then I caught myself in time before Señor Bascon noticed anything. Was there some devil hidden inside of me? I checked myself promptly and regained my composure in spite of the woman's scrutiny.

"Asay!" the man called out. "Where is that girl? Out again in her horse?"

The sound of running feet, and a young woman burst into the room. Or was it a young man? It was wearing a man's loose cotton pants and shirt, too big for its size. It felt familiar, and the next moment

I recognized the girl at the beach, now wearing her long hair tied in a neat bun at the base of her head.

She gave an obvious jolt at the sight of me. Surprise and delight crossed her face, followed by a blush as she lowered her eyes.

"Asay, you have been out on that horse since dawn. Could you not sleep again?" Señor Bascon asked sternly, but his voice betrayed his love for his daughter. "Go, girl, go have some chickens slaughtered, maybe four of them, and bring them to the convento immediately. About time that horse pays for its keep."

"And please go to the vegetable patch and harvest some onions and tomatoes. And don't forget the potatoes and the garlic in our shed. Those chickens will need garnishing," the man added. "The Padre here must feel proud that we natives have acquired some Spanish taste, at last."

I felt my mouth water at the memory of my favorite Spanish tapas, with olives, tomatoes, bacon, chorizo or tuna. With only the coconut juice in my insides, I could think of nothing else but food.

"And shame on you! Go put on some decent clothing," the father lovingly called out to his daughter.

---

[7] *People with mixed blood*
[8] *Good morning. Where are you going?*
[9] *Woman, please have pity*

CHAPTER 3

NICOLASA

It was a hot summer day in May, 1884. I had just been riding out in my horse aimlessly through the fields the entire afternoon. This was the only way I could get some sleep at night. Otherwise, I would lie awake until the break of dawn.

I must be going mad, I told myself. This angst was killing me slowly, softly, like the rain patiently cuts through hard rock and finally breaks it. I felt my horse leading me to the mangrove swamps. It was cool here and I alighted and sat under a coconut tree. Then, I was suddenly overwhelmed by a deep sadness. And I broke into violent sobs, tears of despair running down my cheeks.

Then, a figure loomed in front of me. I was startled to see the parish priest, Padre Antolin, peering down at my face. In the next instant I was up and running away as fast as I could before he recognized me.

Later, he came to our house. He must have been lost. I thought he came to tell [10]*Tatay* and *Nanay* about seeing me at the swamps. But weeks went by and he didn't say a word. Not many people were that [11]*bueno.*

So, there I was - Asay - sitting in that round oak table since morning. Sometimes I would take my eyes off the vestments I was making, and gaze out the wide window of this convento of the Santa Teresa de Avila parish church of Talisay. The sea, the sky, all that blue soothed my tired eyes. The parish had had a dire need for new vestments, and here I sat working at them with utter devotion.

"Nicolasa, you are so good at needlework, and it's time you do something worthwhile with your life instead of galloping away in that little horse of yours. Anyway, you never enjoy raising chickens or planting tomatoes," *Nanay* told me.

But what my mother – poor simple woman – could not admit is that this daughter would not survive without riding her horse for hours. Riding through the fields under the wide blue sky was the only time I could really breathe. Otherwise I would suffocate and die a slow death in this sleepy town. But I had to please my mother - poor woman – what joys did she really get out of life – or so I, the wild daughter, thought.

So here I was, the useless daughter, bent over my needlework. The embroidery of vestments and tapestries, working with delicate threads imported from China, had been my life since Padre Antolin first came to our house exactly a year ago. I got little money for my work, just like all workers in this colony. But at least the food was good. I would take my horse each morning to the convento and come back home long after supper. I could then fall into a sound sleep.

For some unfathomable cause, I had spent much of the past year deprived of sleep. I was ready to die a premature death from sleeplessness. Until I started making the vestments… This work had saved my life.

Darkness would soon descend around me; I should really start for home, I would think. But I could not take my hands off that vestment. My greatest reward was the sight of Padre Antolin wearing them for ceremonies. Then, he looked even more holy, more Godlike.

I would never forget the first time I came inside this convento. Following *Tatay*'s orders, I came on my horse to deliver some chickens for the Padre. But not one of the servants was around to receive them, so I ended up cooking the dishes myself – *pollo frito* - the leanest chicken fried crispy with garlic - chicken *caldereta* stewed in tomatoes with potatoes and sweet pepper, and rice fried in garlic and onions.

My reward - the obvious look of pleasure on Padre Antolin's face as he savored every last morsel!

Ever since then, the Padre would often visit our home, and *Nanay* would ask me to cook a chicken for him. I often wondered why *Nanay* - if she was so devoted to the Padre - why she would not come to the convento and cook for him herself. But that would have stirred some juicy gossip.

Nanay would rather fix herself up in her lace [12]*kimonas* and embroidered [13]*patadyongs*, coiffure her hair, and give a little envelope personally to Padre Antolin after each Sunday mass, just like the matrons of prominent families in this town.

First, the women would sit right in the front pews and gaze up at him in adoration, as he performed the rituals in Latin and deliver the sermon in Binisaya. He sounded so eloquent, so powerful. It surely was that voice.

His voice was deep and husky, and listening to it with my eyes closed, I retreated to a forest dark and cool, enclosed like in a womb.

Then, as the men watched, amused, the women would all flock around him after the ceremonies, *Nanay* in the lead. They would then reward him with little envelopes containing contributions - an excited little group, grateful for the high he provided their otherwise dull lives.

Then my heart would give a little lurch when I heard Padre Antolin's footsteps running up the stairs.

[14]"*Muy bonita,*" he would say, as he fingered my exquisite embroidery. [15]"*Muchas gracias,* Nicolasa." He was clearly impressed.

He had been quite busy with parish duties and came home long after dark. Each morning started with a mass. Then he taught religion, reading, and even arithmetic at the little improvised primary school in the parish compound. Some days he visited the sick, honored invitations, and on weekends, went the rounds of the large friar estates around Talisay and Minglanilla. Lately, he had been helping town officials organize this new town of Talisay. As though all this was not upsetting enough, the *guardias civiles* had been thinning out in number, leaving the parish priest to settle disputes. So, I would wait for him to come home and find me there, at this table by the window, working at my needlework.

I loved to play mother and prepare his dinner.

I expected him to ask me why I was crying that day at the swamps. But he never did. Any other man would have. But he was not just any man. He was very special. A deep respect for him began to sprout in my heart, a seed holding much promise.

Many times, Padre Antolin would give me an extra [16]*parol* as it grew dark.

"Padre, *muchas gracias*," I would say, practicing my Spanish, "but really this extra light is not necessary. We will be wasting the oil."

"Hija, you will destroy your beautiful eyes," he would tell me, half in jest. My small, dark eyes were really very ordinary. "*Bueno,* why don't we share this light? Here I'll sit across from you to do some writing."

And he would bring pen and paper and bend over his work, totally absorbed. Every now and then, he would look up at me, laughing or frowning at his thoughts.

[17]"*Monte bello...monte bello...en el cielo...*" he would mutter under his breath, his eyes far away. "*Cielo*" was a word he often muttered as he wrote. He seemed preoccupied with the idea of "heaven". I often wondered why anyone so young would even think of the afterlife.

I had never seen eyes of that color. The way the brown and green color in his eyes shifted with the light fascinated me. I imagined there was a tiny creature behind the eyes which changed shape and color as it moved. The eyes also seemed to shift with his mood –liquid with sadness, dark with anger, bright with joy – but always with that intense and penetrating look, like he could see right into my soul.

Much later I found that there was indeed a creature hidden inside him, someone who was him but not him. And I was soon to find out what it was. Not without a price.

Our eyes tired, we would sit back and stare out the window at the rising moon.

"My hometown, Castrogeriz, is very far from the sea. Just low hills and plains as far as your eyes can see – a green and gold merging with blue sky," he told me once.

"Why is the land gold?" I asked.

"The wheat – endless wheat fields – and the corn. And the sunflowers – as large as your face..." he made a fist in front of my face. "On a clear day, the land seemed to heave, moving from one direction to the other."

"Are there earthquakes there as well?" I asked.

"No, Hija," he laughed, "the entire field of wheat moves with the wind, making waves just like water, with varying shades of gold."

And his hand would move to mimic the waves, while he whistled softly like the wind. "You should see them," he said wistfully.

I told him I had never seen sunflowers. So he got a little oil portrait he had saved, and showed me a faded painting of a field of sunflowers.

"My mother and I painted this portrait together one summer day when I was but eight years old," he told me proudly, his voice filled with nostalgia.

"It's beautiful. Look at all that gold against the blue sky!" I exclaimed.

"I have longed to see places," I added, holding back tears, "where people do great things."

"You are still so young. Why, you are hardly eighteen, aren't you?" he asked.

The silence which followed was overpowering. Then, I said, "I'm 27 years old, Padre. Like they say, [18] *ulay na gyud*. It should be obvious to everyone who sees me," I admitted, "I'm too old for a lot of things – unless I were really good-looking or wealthy or talented – none of which I am."

I took several deep gulps, trying not to cry.

"Oh, please, Hija. You will certainly still get married to a nice and famous gentleman who will take you places," he tried to soothe me.

"No!!!" I screamed inside me. "I will always be here – in this town, among the chickens, the goats, these fields, our little life – I am stuck here. Will I even have children at all? Will anyone even look at me twice for that to happen?"

But no words came out of my lips. The air around us seemed to crackle with my thoughts.

"I want someone like you," I wanted to say to the man in front of me, "not just any Pablo or Juan or even that old man, Isiong - shame on him making a pass at me - who have never been anywhere and who don't know anything but raising goats and pigs and growing corn, coming to bed smelling of fish and dazed with [19] *tubâ*!"

Then the Padre looked at me like he could see through me. He must have felt me pulsating all over, vibrating from head to toe. Was that why he seemed so sure I would eventually find a man? He said I only needed to go out there. Where, I knew not. I just knew that he could look into my soul, so akin to his own.

And I was right.

"We are kindred spirits," he said. "How sad that indeed this small town has nothing much to offer for one as talented as you."

"Asay, Hija, you and I are so much alike. We have both lived in small farming towns," he added after a brief silence. "But we are unique, Hija. You and I are artists. I see that same creative spark in you. We need creative expression as much or even more than food and shelter."

"More than food and a house, Padre?" I asked, astonished.

"Yes, we were taught so. And I believe so. Without some kind of creative self-expression, a man might very well lose the impetus to work at all," he told me.

"I thought chickens were enough to make you happy," I teased him, and the next moment we were both bent over in hearty laughter. Padre Antolin had been coming over to visit our Bascon household regularly, especially when he was hungry. Each time he came, he would chase the chickens around the backyard. "Choo, choo, choo…choo, choo, choo…" he would call out to them in a singsong voice.

"No chickens, no lunch!" Nanay would tease us.

---

10 *father and mother in Binisaya*
11 *good in Spanish*
12 *Loose native blouse, usually embellished with embroidery*
13 *Native wrap-around skirt*
14 *How beautiful, in Spanish*
15 *Thank you very much, in Spanish*
16 *oil lamp in Binisaya*
17 *beautiful mountain in heaven, in Spanish*
18 *spinster already, in Binisaya*
19 *fermented coconut alcoholic beverage, in Binisaya*

In order to arrive at the Truth, a man finds himself examining the Other Side. Often, without being fully conscious of his actions, he puts his beliefs and practices to a severe test. Other forces around him seem to cooperate by leading him to the people and the places which he needs for the Big Trial.

Around our central character, the Slaves are insidiously revolting against the Master, the Spanish government and especially the Spanish friars.

With his life and sanity severely challenged, our Friar is led to revolt against his Master, his Sacred Vows and Promises.

The Painful Truth is hard to accept as God's Will, and Freedom will come at a high price.

(Inspired by Wilhelm Friedrich Hegel)

DISCUSSION II
The Scholar

"Happy man, eager for life/Tender father of the precious heritage/And cheerful sucking native soil/A pure environment//

"Free from the yoke of petty ambition/Of envy and greed/ Here in the field of sacred innocence/Peace and bliss//

"There, lying on the neighboring hill/Go their flocks in the shady forest/The meek sheep and goats graze/Rich milk//

"It tends to view its fertile plains/And feel the breeze's pulse flutter/Among the rich harvest of golden spike/In gentle waves//

LA VIDA DEL CAMPO, by Antolin Frias y Ramos

"I often come here these days - just to get the feel," I told my sister **Joy** *as we sit with my friend M. and cousin E. around the courtyard at the* **Basilica del Santo Niño**.

"Well, the place should have just the right vibes for your story," she replied.

"*These centuries-old stone walls and arches must harbor its share of ghosts*", M. said. "*Uh, just look up there at that cute little stone balcony. It looks haunted. And that roof garden with the lovely trellis, this antique fountain in the middle of the square – all very cool.*"

"*By the way, I have just finished the translation of* **Fr. Frias' poem**, **'La Vida del Campo'**,*" I told them. "*Now listen!*" And I read the first few stanzas of the poem.*

"*What kind of man would write such poetry?*" asked E.

"*The first stanza makes us imagine a scene so...*" M. groped for the right word.

"*Serene...peaceful,*" I supplied it. "*The peace and bliss of one surrounded by the beauty of nature...*"

"*It is not surprising. That certainly speaks of the town where Fr. Frias was born and bred. He was born in* **Castrogeriz in 1857**. *I should know. I have just gone there,*" my sister Joy said.

Joy had just arrived from a walking pilgrimage, the famous **Camino de Santiago** *in Spain, an 800 km. walk along the northern part of Spain starting from a point in the French border and ending in* **Santiago de Compostela** *where the relic of St. James the Apostle or Santiago is kept in a beautiful cathedral.*

Along the way, she made a stop at the big city of **Burgos**, *from where one bus ride took her to* **Valladolid**. *There, she visited the seminary, the* **Real Seminario de los Padres Agustinos Filipinos**, *where our great grandfather Fr. Frias studied and was ordained as an Augustinian priest. Not far away and also along the Camino de Santiago is the town of* **Castrogeriz**, *Padre Antolin's hometown.*

"*Amazing!*" E. said. "*What's it like there?*"

"*You can imagine it from the pictures. There's a lot of data in the internet,*" I told her. "*All these towns – like Castrogeriz, Valladolid, and others – in the Northern province of* **Castille-Lyon** – *surround the greater city of* **Burgos**.*"

"*In fact, as records show, Fr. Frias's parents,* **Juan and Luisa Frias**, *were born in the neighboring town of* **Torresandino**," *Joy added. "*The entire region is just so full of Frias's that there is even a town there called* **Frias**, *and Google shows a* **Frias coat-of-arms**.*"

"A coat of arms? Does that mean you have noble blood in your veins?" M. said, incredulous.

"Well, not necessarily," I answered with a smile. "Although I wouldn't mind having one, would you? It simply means that the family has grown so large through the generations that they need a family seal, just for distinction."

"So, how did they end up in Castrogeriz?" asked E.

Castrogeriz is strategic as the midpoint in the Camino de Santiago. Still standing to this day is a hospital monastery where sick pilgrims were treated," answered Joy. "Besides, his folks could have made a living running a bed and breakfast for the pilgrims. That in addition to owning large tracts of land to cultivate wheat and raise sheep and horses...Obviously, they were not poor."

*"But," I added, "with Castrogeriz just less than a hundred kms. from the bigger town of **Burgos**, the **Frias family could also have been merchants as well as farmers.** Burgos is famous for its **merchant oligarchy**, being near the border to France and the Bay of Biscay. We have reason to believe that they belonged to the upper class. Would an affluent family like theirs lead a limited life in a small village like Castrogeriz instead of immersing themselves in a richer culture in cosmopolitan Burgos?"*

"Seeing how small Castrogeriz is in the pictures, the Frias's would most probably have the best of both worlds - live in Burgos while running a farm in nearby Castrogeriz, as well," someone suggested.

"And with all those horses and that large open space, the young Frias would have galloped away across the endless wheat and corn fields towards the horizon," I suggested. "The astounding sunsets would have made a contemplative out of him."

*"**Here, in the shade, in the flowery grass/And on the banks of the silvery river/I live cheerful without hearing the echoes/The Vain world...**" I read further from the LA VIDA DEL CAMPO.*

"He would have been deprived of a view of the ocean for long periods. On rare occasions, his family might have traversed the long distances on a coach to take a holiday in the Atlantic Coast," I speculated.

"**Padre Antolin's school records** *shows that he was sent to an exclusive boy's boarding school before he entered the seminary,*" *Joy told me once more.* "*His family must have been well-do-do, obviously.*"

Joy actually saw the school records of Padre Antolin at Valladolid, now yellowed and frayed with age.

"*I wonder if this was at the* **Colegio la Vid** *where he wrote his poem* '*La Vida del Campo*' *as well as his other work,* '**Memoria**,'" *I speculated.* "*Before entering the Seminary, the boys had to study for the novitiate in a monastery. The present day La Vid, a few kilometers from Valladolid, used to be a monastery with a colegio, but now it is just a monastery. You should watch it on You-tube – such natural and architectural beauty. And the pictures flashed to beautiful music - flute. It sounds like magic. The show haunted me for days. This is the 'campo' that Padre Antolin writes about in his poem.*"

"*Ah, does that mean he did not have much fun in his teens – no parties, no girls? That in itself tells a story,*" *M. wondered.*

"*Well, he was* **a serious and brilliant student,** *according to the comments his professors noted in his student records. He was also* **a writer,** *who contributed regularly to their school publication,*" *Joy said.*

"*A real nerd,*" *said M.*

"*The seminary records reflect Fr. Frias's parents' names:* ***JUAN FRIAS and LUISA RAMOS FRIAS.*** *There are no siblings listed. When he entered the seminary at the age of seventeen, his mother, Luisa Ramos, was listed as deceased,*" *she added.*

"*A later investigation that I made at the Family Search.com of the Mormons here in Cebu revealed that he had a sister,* **Olimpia,**" *I told them about my trip to the Mormon Temple.* "*She was born when Antolin was ten-years-old, so he must have lost his mother between the ages of ten and seventeen. That might explain why his father sent him to boarding school,*" *I put two and two together.*

"*That would have contained the adolescent well after his mother's early death. The boarding school would also have provided him with a well-regimented life, not much different than one in a seminary.*"

"*Being a writer, his sensitive nature would have reacted to the early loss of his mother drastically,*" M. said.

"*He was ordained and vested the* **Profesion Religiosa in 1876** *and became a priest at the young age of nineteen.*" Joy added.

"*That is just so shockingly young for one to take such serious, lifetime vows – a priest forever!*" said E.

"*All these in an idealistic and serious youth - living in an isolated town of Castrogeriz in the mid 1800's, an early education in nearby city of Burgos, losing one's mother at an early age, the urgent need for priests in the far-flung colonies – combined with an independent and adventurous streak - would have pushed the man Antolin Frias in only one direction – to be a missionary in the colonies.*"

"*A turning point – leading to paths less travelled. He chose that road – the rough one. Imagine living in the colonies in those days. All the challenges they had to face – the journey from Spain to the Philippines, even in* **the more modern steamboats,** *took* **six weeks** *through rough seas.*"

"*Then came the time to depart for the colonies. Like all parents, his father was told that if his son left for colonies, he might never see him again,*" Joy said further.

"*Wow! I could not imagine not seeing Danny ever again,*" M. said of her son.

"*And there would have been this young priest on a boat. It would have been the usual steamship* **from Barcelona** *or* **Marseilles to Manila** *– a six-week-long journey through the rough, perilous seas and the Indian Ocean,*" I shared what I just found at the internet.

"*The steam engine had just been initiated ten years before his journey, a big improvement from the earlier ships with oars and sails which sailed at the mercy of the wind. Nevertheless, the journey even on a steamship was rough and long. One can picture Frias' difficult journey by reading accounts of other journeys of the time, for instance, that of our national hero, Dr. Jose Rizal, from Manila to Barcelona. Frias' journey could not have been much different.*"

"**Simple soul on whom at birth the aurora shone/His prayer rises to subsidiary heaven!!/Never obtrusive nor crying in pain/Happy** *man of his homeland/The pure air and aromas suck!/In camps he offers his soul/Peace and bliss!"* I read further.

"*This 'simple soul' finally found his niche among the 'indios' in the colony. I can safely say now — he did a great job!"* I told them.

"*Life here demanded so much from the friars. Even as late as the 1800's, the friars acted as priests, civic leaders, arbiters, teachers, tax collectors, and judges. They even supervised the building of roads, ports, forts, and other infrastructure,"* I shared what I had read at the University of San Carlos Filipiniana library.

"*The friars also introduced western art and music and western musical instruments. The Filipinos' favorite was singing in the choir. It seems the natives had naturally good voices. Of course, friar abuses are also well-known. There was unpaid labor, land grabbing, and immoral practices resulting in broken homes. But, scholars have found that only a minority of the friars was guilty of such abuses. The rest were really good, productive men."*

"*But the friar orders in the Philippines acquired wealth by owning large tracts of land called haciendas or friar estates. With wealth comes power — always known to corrupt the strongest of men. It's a wonder then that a majority of the friars remained uncorrupted. Sad that it's the glaring minority, the [20] Damaso's, which got immortalized."*

"*A man who does not abuse his power is rare,"* M. said. "*Would Padre Antolin have belonged to that category — a man unaffected by his power?"*

"*Ah, that's a question I've been weighing in my mind for many years now. Records from the archives at San Agustin Church in Intramuros reveal his written works on profound topics, such as history and civilization. He would have had too much integrity to abuse his power,"* I answered.

"*But what strikes me most,"* I continued, "*is his poetry, 'La Vida del Campo'. Poetry is special. When one writes a poem he must think in metaphors — that is, in symbols and beautiful imagery. One should be capable of looking beneath the surface to write a good poem."*

A long silence followed as we sank deep in our own thoughts.

"At any rate, Padre Antolin was certainly not the type who would call a spade a spade. He would say something like [21] 'My love is like a red, red rose'," *M. said.*

"Or," I answered, [22] "the world in a grain of sand...infinity in a flower...". *We all laugh a little.*

"So, can we think of him as the artist who had too much integrity to steal what did not belong to him?"

I reflected on our discussion for a long minute. Meanwhile, we enjoyed eating [23] hopia *and* siopao.

"Creative energy is a tremendous responsibility," M. added. *"Sad that many parents and society as a whole have neglected their artistic children – resulting in so much frustration".*

"The same frustration which sometimes results in promiscuity or drug addition?" I asked. "Okay, I've been watching too many movies. But that's a good point and one which we can probably use to understand a lot of bad behavior...But not to excuse it..."

"Whatever! It seems the rural folk in Frias' day and time was only concerned with basics. Still, no matter what he did, our Padre would have acted from his heart. Power and greed would not be his corruptor," we all agreed.

"It seems we have all done our homework! We all sound very correct. None of us is an expert here. But, of course, we can have our educated guesses," Joy said.

"Just points to ponder on," I told them.

---

[20] *A character in Noli me Tangere, a historical novel by Philippine National Hero, Dr. Jose Rizal*

[21] *lines from the poem A RED, RED ROSE by Robert Burns*

[22] *lines from the poem AUGURIES OF INNOCENCE by Gerald Manley Hopkins*

[23] *Chinese dumplings*

VALLADOLID, a city not far from Burgos, in the northern province of Castile-Lyon, was once a royal capital, where the King and Queen of Spain sought refuge from Moorish rule in the 1100's. In 1743, after the Augustinian order was established in the Philippine colony, King Felipe V of Spain ordered the construction of a seminary to train priests for the Philippines and other colonies. This turned out to be the REAL SEMINARIO DE LOS PADRES AGUSTINOS FILIPINOS.

Real Colegio de los Padres Agustinos Filipinos in Valladolid, Spain

Joy B. Regner at the seminary which her great grandfather Antolin Frias attended

JOY B. REGNER – VALLADOLID, SPAIN

Photo Courtesy of Joy B. Regner

CATHEDRAL OF ST. MARY

Burgos, Spain

Built in the 13th century

Photo courtesy of Joy B. Regner

BURGOS, a city in Burgos province in Northern Spain, is located at the edge of the Iberian central plateau, known as the Meseta, with a population of 200,000. It is the historic capital of the province of Castille, and was once the seat of the Crown of Castile.

Since the 11th century, the city has been situated in the principal crossroads of Northern Spain, along the famed pilgrimage route, the Camino de Santiago. Due to its proximity to the Bay of Biscay and the border with Southern France, the city has also been a crossroads for merchants and overseas trade, giving rise to a strong merchant oligarchy.

Having been the scene of numerous wars for centuries, the area around Burgos is dotted with castles built for its defense. The little towns in its suburbs, like CASTROGERIZ and FRIAS TOWN and other small charming towns, lie in windswept plains dotted by wheat, sunflower fields, and vineyards for wine production. The once royal city of VALLADOLID is just an hour's drive away.

Due to its inland location and high altitude, Burgos and its environs is very cold and windy in the winter and hot in the summers.

The early inhabitants of this part of Spain were Celtic, Roman, Visigots, and Celtiberians.

Main Altar at the Colegio de los Padres Agustinos Filipinos, Valladolid, Spain

RUINS OF THE OLD SEMINARY AT THE ST. AGUSTIN
CHURCH COMPOUND IN INTRAMUROS, MANILA

San Agustin Church in Manila built in 1607

The Order of Saint Augustine

The Order of Saint Augustine started out in the 8th century as a group of hermits led by St. Augustine of Hippo. They followed the Rule of St. Augustine on the monastic life, which primarily prohibited the ownership of private property. Around the 11th century these groups went their separate ways and spread themselves throughout Italy. In the 13th century the Holy See ordered these groups to congregate as one Order. Hence, the Order of Saint Augustine was officially founded, with goals toward learning, science, and missionary work. Their apostolate spread around the globe in the age of exploration and colonization from the 1500's until the 1900's.

The OSA was the first Christian missionaries to arrive in the Philippines with Ferdinand Magellan in March, 1521, a mission which was short-lived. In 1565 Miguel Lopez de Legaspi and his fleet landed in Cebu to colonize the Philippines together with Fr. Andres de Urdaneta, OSA, and the first house of the OSA was founded in Cebu soon after they landed, in the site where the Basilica del Santo Niño now stands. The miraculous image of the Santo Niño (the Infant Jesus of Prague) which was originally given by Magellan to the native Queen Juana in 1521, eventually found its home in the Basilica.

On Dec. 31, 1575, Fr. Andres de Urdaneta established the first permanent Spanish settlement in the Philippines at the San Agustin Church and Monastery in Manila, and named it the Augustinian Province of the Most Holy Name of Jesus of the Philippines.

The Spanish Friars, especially the Augustinians, suffered persecution in the Philippines at the end of the 19th century. By this time, the OSA had 225 parishes with 2,237,743 souls, 400 schools and churches, 328 village missions.

At the present time, the OSA owns several major educational institutions in the Philippines, one of which is the University of San Agustin in Iloilo City. Their major churches include the Basilica del Sto. Nino in Cebu and the San Agustin Church in Manila.

Basilica del Sto. Niño de Cebu

THE SANTO NINO, miraculous statue given as a gift
by Ferdinand Magellan to Rajah Humabon in 1521,
now found at the Basilica del Santo Nino in Cebu

CHAPTER 4

—— ❁ ——

THE REVELATION

One early afternoon after lunch Padre Antolin was summoned to a nearby farm to perform the last rites on a woman who was dying. Having failed to find Dodong, the sacristan, he asked me - Asay - to leave my needlework to assist him. Carrying his white habit and the paraphernalia, we walked across the sugar cane fields for a mile.

As we approached the house, we heard the sound of weeping women. I noticed Padre Antolin clutching at his stomach, all tense. But then with a deep breath, he seemed to be gathering strength for the task before him.

The house was a large nipa structure, surrounded by coconut trees. Just as we approached it, a woman came down the bamboo steps. As she passed, Padre Antolin glanced at the pail that she was carrying. It was filled with what looked like fresh blood. His face drained of color, he had to hold on to my arm for support. The air around us was heavy with impending rain, and the oppressive air made it hard for one to breathe. I was quick to sense his distress and held his hand in a tight grasp. In no time, he recovered from his shock, and we both entered the house to face whatever horror awaited us.

The stench – of blood, sweat, dirty linen – assailed our nostrils. Padre Antolin struggled hard not to cover his nose. A woman lay in bed, covered with bloody sheets up to her neck. The lips in the pale face had turned blue at the corners. Four other women sat around her, weeping. One of them was carrying a bundle covered with a blanket. It had the shape of an infant, its tiny face barely visible.

By the window sat a young man, around his mid-thirties. He held his head in his hands. No sound came from him. I looked around the room and saw a little boy of about seven crouching behind the door, his eyes filled with fear.

"I am the mother," the older of the women managed to blurt out. Her sobs tore at my heart. She inhaled deeply and said, "My daughter delivered this baby girl before daybreak. The [24] *inunlan* never came out. She has not stopped bleeding all this time."

"They summoned me," said another woman, who seemed to be a midwife, "but there was nothing I could do. She needed a good doctor, but it is too late now."

Padre Antolin still looked pale and nauseated and looked like he was about to throw up his breakfast. I had a sense of an old unhealed wound opening up in him. I was sure he just felt like running as fast as he could away from this horror, this darkness. But instead he took several deep breaths. I just knew he would muster enough strength to elevate himself above all emotion. Then he started to give the woman the sacrament of Extreme Unction.

Meanwhile, I took the bundled infant from the woman, who gave a deep sigh, now that her arm could finally rest. I carried the infant to a chair by the window for air, and held it close to me during the ceremony. I inhaled the baby's sweet aroma, savored it with my eyes closed, and immediately felt a renewed vigor.

"If only this were my child…"

I had inhaled the aroma of babies many times before, but just then this baby smelled sweeter than any of them. Something magical had happened to me. My senses had become sharpened ever since…yes, since I started spending more time with Padre Antolin. He seemed to have cast a spell on me.

With his sacred duties done, Padre Antolin approached the man who had all this time remained in his corner.

"I am so sorry," he said, his hand on the man's shoulders, "And it's alright to weep, to cry it all out. We all need to cry out our pain."

He sounded like one who had known what pain meant. And I could hardly wait to hear his story.

As Padre Antolin and I walked back towards the convento in absolute silence, engrossed in deep thought, it started to drizzle, and we ran for shelter in a nearby stable. Inside we found a few goats, one a horned muscular male and two clearly pregnant females. The fourth was a little white kid.

[25]"Ah, *que bonito!*" Padre Antolin exclaimed, catching the kid in his arms. "Look at this beauty – it is almost entirely white. Ah, it reminds me of the little lambs we had in Castrogeriz."

His voice was sad and hoarse with suppressed tears. Around us, the rain whispered. I did not say a word, offering refuge with my quiet presence.

"Nicolasa, your beauty is not something you would see in the mirror," I heard him say,"you shine from deep within your soul. I was struck by the way you held the little infant earlier, light emanating from your face".

"Hija, you would make a perfect mother!" he announced, his voice ringing with the excitement of one who has finally arrived at an answer, "and you should have a lot of children. And that wonderful lilt in your voice – I almost envy the children who will bask in your lullabies."

I finally managed an awkward smile. "Is this all a dream?" I thought.

"You have an enigmatic smile," he continued, "I have seen it before. I grew up with a reproduction of a painting called 'Mona Lisa' hanging in our wall. My father and I enjoyed guessing what the smile meant - she had a secret lover, or she was expecting a child, or she won the lottery."

"I am going to have your child," I decided quietly. I bowed my head like one making a sacred vow. Even I was surprised at my own thoughts. It frightened me. "Afterwards, you can forget about me. It is final."

I remember clutching my arms tightly across my chest as a sensation of heat crept up in me.

"I lost my mother when I was only ten years old" he said, as the rain fell gently around us, "she died giving birth to twins – a boy and a girl. The boy died as well, but the baby girl lived. The boy we baptized

Jose. And the girl, my sister, was named Olimpia. Of the three, she was the winner."

"My mother's name was Luisa," he went on "She was a sensitive and artistic woman…you remember that portrait of the sunflower I showed you? We both painted that one summer afternoon. But she was very frail. After the sad event, nothing was ever the same again in our family. It took a very long time for my father, Juan, to recover from the loss."

I listened, absorbed in his words. These moments in the stable vibrated with that magic which surrounds epiphanies - my decision to be the mother of his child, and now his revelation of a long-held precious secret.

"My father became quiet and despondent. He stopped playing with me. He would just look at me for long periods, as though looking for something in me. Then he finally picked himself up and started to work long hours in the farm, his head bent over milking cows and planting potatoes."

"Soon after, he sent me to an exclusive boy's boarding school in the nearby city of Burgos. I was an [26] *interno*. I went home only on some weekends. I always believed he did that to get me out of the way. It proved providential. I began to have fun in the school. I made lots of friends, and the priests gave us a lot of love and attention. I also learned good habits, like cleanliness."

"After you lost your mother, this life as an *interno* was exactly what you needed," I said.

"You understand it so well, Asay. The life as an *interno* was regimented and predictable. Most of all, I felt protected there," the Padre replied.

"Ah, so is that why you decided to enter the priesthood?" I asked.

"Oh yes, as a young teenage boy, I thought that was the safest thing to do. Besides, after my mother died, I was told that she had gone to heaven," he said, sounding like he could be talking more to himself.

A heavy downpour suddenly threatened to drown out his words, as though the world did not want to hear what he had to say.

"And the surest path to get to heaven was for me to become a priest!!" he shouted at the top of his voice to beat the din the rain made on the tin roof.

I laughed hard. He sounded so dramatic. But he only looked at me strangely, wondering what provoked my laughter.

"This gave my father renewed hope," he went on, still shouting, "Priests were urgently needed for the colonies. The Augustinian seminary was right in Valladolid, a city not far from Castrogeriz. My life was then sealed."

"Ah, so this is why he always mentions heaven," I thought.

"Then my father met a woman who transformed our big house into an inn. Things began to look up again for him after that," he continued.

"An inn in the middle of wheat and sunflower fields?" I asked.

"Oh, yes. An inn for [27] *peregrinos*. Burgos and Castrogeriz have been stops on the pilgrimage to Santiago de Compostela. Castrogeriz, being midway in the 800-mile pilgrim's walk, is where the pilgrims reached a point of exhaustion and succumbed to illness, especially the dreaded St. Anthony's Fire. So until the present day, there are the remnants of an old hospital there owned and run by the famous Order of St. Anthony. This is where I grew up. Someday, I shall tell you more about this pilgrimage," he answered.

"I became a priest. By then, my father had married the same woman who managed our inn. Another woman had taken my mother's place in our home. I was just eager to go as far away as possible."

"The Seminario de los Padres Agustinos Filipinos was established in Valladolid by the royalty to train priests especially for the colonies."

"'You might never see your son again, once he gets on that boat to Las Islas Filipinas'," the headmaster told my father before I was admitted."

"So what did your father say?"

"For a while, he brooded over it. But my father had been a devout Christian. The idea of the Eternal had been pounded on him. Everything in this world was a preparation for the end goal, which is heaven."

"And what happened to your sister, Olimpia?" I asked.

"I heard that she has married a nice man, Fernando Alonso, and had a big wedding in Valladolid. They have a son, Juan, named after my father."

The rain had stopped. Breathing in the air, now fragrant with the musky smell of coconuts, we slowly walked back to the convento.

"I had a horse in Spain. His name was Juanito," he told me, laughing. "I miss him now as I talk about home."

"So you went riding there, too?" I asked, relieved at the happier note in his voice.

"It was a dire necessity. Around Burgos and the surrounding towns, a horse was the only way we could go around. The wheat and corn fields and pastures stretched out endlessly across the hills and valleys."

A bell rang in my head.

"I have an idea," I heard myself say, "why don't I go riding with you around the haciendas? I can help you deal with the tenants – as best through their wives."

"That's the best thing I've heard in a long time," he said, obvious relief in his voice, "women have cooler heads when it comes to setting conflicts. I have not heard from some of the tenants in the haciendas for months now. My visits there are long overdue."

The next day, I brought my sister, Eustaquia, to the convento. Yayang was older than I by two years. She had been chasing chickens with Padre Antolin and me in our backyard. She had also been doing floral arrangements for the church. But singing in the church choir was where she excelled the most.

But unlike me, she did not think of herself as forgotten "on the shelf". Hope shone through her slanted eyes, and her sensuous lips seemed forever on the verge of laughter. With the same native features, she was just as tall and fair as I was, but she looked more voluptuous, with wider hips and fuller breasts. That's what everyone said about her.

"Padre, Yayang is very good at needlework, even better than I am," I told Padre Antolin, "she can take over the vestments while we go out riding."

"Perfect!" he said happily.

---

[24] *placenta*
[25] *how beautiful*
[26] *boarder*
[27] *pilgrims*

CHAPTER 5

=======　❀　=======

HACIENDAS DE TALISAY

July, 1884. The season of the monsoon rains found me and Asay riding together almost every day to make the rounds of the haciendas. We must have been a sight to behold, in our loose muslin pants and shirt, I on a black stallion and she on a brown mare.

The haciendas covered an area of 8,100 hectares, stretching from the mountainous areas all the way to the sea - seemingly boundless fields of sugar cane, corn, coconuts, and bananas dotted with stables for livestock, beyond which were rice fields and mangrove swamps lining the seashore. The land covered the entire towns of Talisay and Minglanilla, and they were all rented out to tenants. The main road heading towards the south of the province ran through the town in the middle of the haciendas.

Running across the fields from the hills were several rivers. One of them, called Linao, was notorious for flooding - even with just one heavy rain - inundating the road and forming a large lake in the low-lying areas. There were flash floods, when the water rose abruptly without warning, which washed away people, especially children, and livestock out to sea."

That day was just like any other – or so I thought. We were due to visit a tenant in an *hacienda* in Minglanilla. I had not heard from him for months, and his rental was overdue.

"Manoy Sidro has nine children, am I right?" I asked Asay.

"I don't know them all that well," she answered. "From what I hear, his wife has always been sick. She has a growth in her throat which keeps getting bigger, and she stays in bed most of the time."

"I seem to have heard that one of his grown sons went berserk and burned their nipa house," I said. "I regret I could not attend to the problem immediately. They should have called the *guardias civiles*. But, God help me, where have the *guardias* gone? There's hardly any left in this town."

"This has always been a problem in this colony – the population is too widely dispersed. This makes it harder to control," I added.

As we approached the property, we saw a man walking towards us through the sugar cane fields. I immediately recognized Sidro's quick, easy strides.

[28]*Maayong buntag*, Sidro," I greeted him. [29] "*Como estas tu, mi amigo?*"

"*Buenas diaz*, Padre," Sidro answered with a big smile. "*Maayong buntag*. What do you think of my Spanish? This is a nice surprise. You have not visited us for a few months now."

He was wearing loose muslin pants and shirt which looked like they were once flour sacks.

[30] "*Si, lo siento*. I have been so busy lately," I explained, "This is Asay, one of my assistants."

Asay and I alighted from our horses into the wet grass.

[31] "*Buenas diaz*, Señor Sidro," Nicolasa greeted the man.

"*Buenas, Senorita…*" Sidro greeted her back.

[32] "*Yo soy Nicolasa*," she answered in her lilting voice, tossing back her long hair, proud of her Spanish. Both natives laughed merrily at each other.

Sidro gave Nicolasa an intent look. It seemed like he felt the air pulsating around the young woman – the joy which I myself didn't fail to notice.

"She is a woman in love," I quietly admitted to myself, "and the man can see it." Then he looked at me more closely, but I was sure he saw nothing but peace in my face.

All three of us started walking along the edge of the large sugar cane fields. In the distance were corn fields surrounded by coconut and banana trees and beyond them the sheds for the goats and the horses.

"Ay, Padre, life for us has been so hard," the man said. "First, Tonio, my eighteen-year-old son, went berserk and burned our house. No one from the guardia civil came, so we had to restrain him with ropes. Then he got better and we breathed a little, but after a time he suddenly went mad again and we had to tie him up once more."

We walked all the way through the coconut trees towards what looked like a makeshift nipa structure.

"See over there is a temporary dwelling to replace the one we lost in the fire," the man says.

[33] *"Muy pequeño!* How could any family fit in there? With all the nipa and hardwood around, I can't see why you can't build a larger structure," I told him.

"Ah, there's just no one to help me do it, Padre. Almost all of my children have left. Four are out working in the Ciudad, and three for Señor Pedro."

I gave a start at the name. Señor Pedro was the encomendero who owned the neighboring hacienda. Officially, this land lay in the next town of Naga, which was outside the boundary of Minglanilla and out of my jurisdiction. Nevertheless, I had established a relationship with Señor Pedro and his family, visiting them whenever I happened to be nearby.

"Señor Pedro? Your children work for him? Sidro, don't you remember how this Señor Pedro treated your neighbors' children last year? The poor young men had bruises in their backs. They were also emaciated and penniless. Pedro gives his laborers a pittance and rotten food for backbreaking work," I said, my voice filled with sadness.

Manoy Sidro looked down at his feet. His silence said it all.

"Alright, Sidro, I'll go visit Pedro tomorrow. Let's hope I will see your children in his farm so I can check them out," I promised. "Meanwhile, what have you got here, Sidro? I see you have expanded the piggery. One can smell pig dung for miles around you – although I don't mind it if it means food for us all. And the bananas trees have grown thicker around the fields. I also notice more coconuts trees, and that they have been bared of nuts. And where are the other carabaos? The last time I was here there were four of them."

Sidro looked down at the ground. "Two carabaos died. They ate grass which was infested by this deadly caterpillar," he muttered under his breath.

"What?!" I exclaimed, "two carabaos? But why didn't you send someone to inform me? I would have ordered the animals contained inside a fenced area. Then they would not have to roam around too far."

Sidro kept his eyes downcast. "Padre, your overseer Simeon has not been here for quite some time now. I heard he has gone deeper into those mountains. Do you know what's going on there, Padre?"

"No, Sidro, but I certainly have an idea," I answered. "I am not as blind as you people think I am. I have also heard reports that someday you natives will murder us Spaniards in our sleep."

Sidro tried to hide the guilt in his face.

"But now let's go back to the carabaos. What you're telling me is a lie, Sidro," I told him gently.

I had been in this situation so many times that I expected to find it every time I visited the haciendas. Theft was obviously one of the main reasons why the haciendas were losing money. With all the gambling and drinking around, the money earned hardly reached the landowners, in this case, us friars.

"Sidro," I said, in a tone one would use for young children, "the rule says that you tenants must inform the owner – us – of everything that happens in your territory. You must also report any additional areas you develop."

[34] "*Pasaylo-a*, Padre," the man humbly answered, "I know we tenants should pay more rent for each additional area cultivated. But if you want to see where I have buried the two carabaos, I can take you there."

"No, *gracias*, Sidro. It's too late to mourn the carabaos now", I answered.

"Ay, Padre, life for us has been very difficult. [35] *Maluoy intawon ka kanamo*, Padre. We poor people have to survive. The river gets flooded even with the slightest rain. And there have been typhoons with very strond winds. You know what that means for the crops."

"Yes, I understand perfectly, Sidro," I said, "but the rule must be followed. The proper thing to do would be to inform the owner, and humbly ask the owner to exempt you from the additional rentals. The owner has the right to know the truth, and we must respect that. Hiding things from the owner would be dishonest."

Sidro's face was flushed with shame. In sympathy, rain clouds began to gather and a clap of thunder reinforced my message.

"Sidro, please do not worry about the rentals. Come to the convent and we will compute what's overdue. Then, you can pay it slowly," I told him gently. "And bring the wife with you. We'll try to attend to her ailment."

"And now," I said the inevitable, "where is that delicious *tuba* of yours? And please go slaughter some chickens and roast them for our lunch." I always gave myself a pat in the stomach to put a strong message across.

"Padre, there's a lot of chickens running around. How would you like to chase one of two of them? I have been told you love the sport," Sidro said in jest.

Asay and I were soon running around a little yard to chase the chickens for our lunch, while Sidro fetched fresh tuba.

"Choo, choo, choo, choo," off we went.

"If only all Spaniards were like you, Padre," Sidro said while we savored the chicken and the *tuba*. "You do not really know the whole story between that Señor Pedro and my family, do you?" he asked.

"A century ago," he went on, "my ancestors were tenants of part of the land which Pedro now occupies in Naga. Through the succeeding decades, Señor Pedro's ancestors gradually encroached beyond their boundaries into our area. The family's protests were drowned by the scare tactics used to threaten them with their lives".

The farmer closed his eyes at the full impact of the memory. "And Pedro's ancestors wanted more; they had to have the women as well. Poverty led some of my female ancestors to work in the encomienda's villa as househelpers. One of them went mad after she was raped and gave birth to an unwanted child. A good number of my cousins are descended from Pedro's ancestors. But all this time, all they got from the encomienda was nothing but seeds blown by the wind."

---

[28] *good morning in Binisaya*
[29] *how are you, my friend? In Spanish*
[30] *Yes, I am sorry, in Spanish*
[31] *Good morning, in Spanish*
[32] *I am Nicolasa*
[33] *How tiny!*
[34] *pardon, in Binisaya*
[35] *Please have mercy on us, in Binisaya*

CHAPTER 6

THE ENCOMENDERO

I sat at my dinner table, feasting on roasted pork and paella. I always ate with gusto, oblivious of all else, including my wife. Now, she was sitting right across from me, like a fixture. I had stopped looking in her direction a long time ago, at the dinner table, in the bedroom, and everywhere else. Instead, I had engrossed myself on the more palatable young woman of the day – there was always someone new every couple of months – the haciendas were full of burgeoning adolescents sent over to me to work in my household. Little did their mothers know – or did they in fact encourage it – how much their daughters satiated my older man's appetite. Yes, this was my way of keeping young, of staying alive, in this land which God seemed to have forgotten. I was getting very old and very lonely...

This hacienda was acquired in the early 1600's by my ancestor who was a soldier in the Spanish army. In those early days when the Philippine colony had just been established, a royal deed gave the Spanish soldiers the option to pick land to own and cultivate. My military ancestor chose a beautiful spot in a large clearing between the hills of Naga, right beside a little narrow river, where he planted coconut trees and corn and raised chickens, cows, and goats in a hundred hectare area.

But at this point, the area had doubled, and it is commonly believed it was done through dubious transactions. My family had been known for grabbing the surrounding land from their native tenants. I could not care less how it was acquired. What mattered was that I was now here, enjoying all this bounty, and nobody would ever take this from me, ever.

I, Señor Pedro del Monte, a wealthy Spanish [36] *haciendero*, was invincible in this colony, Las Islas Filipinas.

Today, Padre Antolin and a woman came to see me. I was surprised how their horses had made the steep climb up the hills. I guess they must have maneuvered themselves along the river beds. An excellent horseman, this Padre! But what really amazed me was the woman, riding on a horse like a regular man.

"Don Pedro, *Ola!*" the padre greeted me with the usual warmth, [37]"*Que tal, amigo? Como estas?*"

We Spaniards embraced warmly. Then I noticed the woman. She seemed uncomfortable, like she was holding her breath. I was suddenly conscious that I had not bathed in days. To her, I must have looked the balding older man with the typical bulge around the middle, my dirty muslin shirt drenched in sweat. I did not understand her reaction. Other women found my body odor irresistible. She looked at me like I were some kind of pig.

"Ah, this time of the year – it is so hot and humid all around," I tried to explain to this snotty character.

Later, sitting across each other over cold drinks of pineapple juice in a large veranda, the priest implored me to let the children of Sidro go.

"I need those boys to work for me at the parish," Padre Antolin told me.

"Padre, with all this rain, this is the time for planting. I need as many men as possible. It would be difficult for me, if not impossible, to let anyone go," I pleaded, scratching my balding head.

Around us, the breezes from the sea sighed through the coconut trees.

Asay sat at a safe distance listening to every word. Her tension was almost palpable. She must have seen Padre Antolin lose his temper and praying it would not happen here. She certainly would have heard about my famous colorful vendettas.

"Pedro, *mi amigo*, I am short of men myself. We have to make furniture for the classrooms. The students have been sitting on the floor for a while now. And Sidro's children are really the best craftsmen in town," Padre Antolin told me.

"Really? I'm surprised to hear that. All these natives seem indolent and almost useless to me," I argued, my ears growing hot.

"Oh, is that why you give them [38] *tahop* to eat, the pounded kernels of corn, food fit only for goats? Is that why you work them to death for a pittance?" the Padre replied, careful to keep his voice at the lowest key.

"That's a big lie! They are not only lazy, they are also liars and cheats – all of them!" I screamed. I felt my face turn red and sweaty.

"Then I am doing you a big favor by taking them off your hands," the Padre replied, calm and cold like one of those statues in his church.

"But what of the girl? She has to help in the kitchen," I asked, referring to Sidro's daughter. "Surely she can't do anything about the furniture."

"She has to attend to her mother who is very sick," the Padre answered. "*Bueno*, I expect the children home with Sidro before sundown today. And thank you for the pineapple drinks. You must have sent the pineapple all the way from Leyte. Well, Pedro, we must go. I expect to see you at the Good Friday procession. [39] *Tu y todas las familias, que?* Doña Carmen, that beautiful wife of yours will enjoy the pageantry."

I gazed at the Padre and the woman as they rode away. With Padre Antolin always checking on us, encomenderos, those indolent natives could get away with murder.

---

[36] *landlord of huge tracts of land*
[37] *how are you, my friend, in Spanish*
[38] *rough coating of pounded corn grain*
[39] *You and the rest of your family, in Spanish*

Evelyn Regner Seno

<u>**Equilibrium is attained by bringing Order out of the Chaos of two opposing forces. – the Thesis and the Antithesis.**</u>

<u>**In our story, our central character's Impulses and Desires have threatened his Social and Moral Commitments. He struggles towards a Synthesis, at the Truth which would set him Free.**</u>

<u>**The Synthesis is in the Hands of God.**</u>

(Inspired by the philosophy of Wilhelm Friedrich Hegel)

DISCUSSION III
The Grand Rebellion

"I can feel an **antithesis** coming," M. said. "Must everyone go through an antithesis before a resolution - the **synthesis** – is reached? I wonder."

"According to **Hegel**, one must examine the Other Side of the entire picture before he can resolve his conflicts," I answered. "This is the time when an individual experiments with one solution or the other, including those not condoned by his society or by his higher self. This he may do with full consciousness or in a spirit of self-deception."

"An entire society may, in fact, go through the same process, for instance, through changes in the entire system of government," M. suggested, "as in a revolution, for instance."

We were sitting by the Church plaza in Talisay, feasting on barbecue and puso, rice wrapped in banana leaves. Behind us loomed the **Church of Sta. Teresa de Avila**, where young Frias first served as parish priest.

"Well said, M." I replied. "My blessed ancestor must go a long way before he passes on his hazel eyes. Before anything is resolved, he must first question his beliefs and experience an Antithesis."

"Is there a book like 'Idiot's Hegel'? This is all way above me" asked E.

"People's lives are determined by the moods and swings of the times, as world history will show" I continue. "...the grand rebellion, then the

61

ultimate resolution. All part of the freedom fight, both for the individual and the society in which he lives."

"Now I am beginning to dig into your guy Hegel. That philosophy is behind what you might call a **catharsis** *- a stunning revelation – which may end up in an* **epiphany***, a new beginning. For instance, a relationship turns sour or stale, needing a closer look, and then the letting go and the starting over."*

"But before the final letting go, your world turns upside down for a moment there, and at this point you might have to do something drastic – the antithesis of all you believe in – like going out with the wrong crowd, for instance."

"Sounds like a really old story."

"The **late nineteenth century in the Philippines** *posed so many problems for the friars. The natives were getting increasingly rebellious. But the rebellion stayed underground and expressed itself in the form of sabotage – like china broken on purpose, to say the least. All this only added to Fray Antolin's personal crisis."*

"So it would seem that the **individual antithesis or personal rebellion** *is aggravated by social factors – all forces around the man driving him towards it, as though he himself wished for them to happen, although this wish would have been submerged in an unconscious level. How Freudian!"*

"Or, rather, **Jungian. Carl Jung** *believed that each one of us has a hidden part called the* **'shadow'***. This is the part of our personality which we have repressed or denied expression. Remember, M., how those nuns in highschool tickled our conscience. Holding a boy's hands a sin, dancing too close a sin, impure thoughts, blah, blah…why, so many girls in their teens simply decided to get married rather than date around for fear of eternal damnation!"*

"Well, I guess we in that generation had so much shadow to deal with. The pretentiousness was sickening. Is that why you used to wash your hands almost every half-hour, M.?"

"At any rate, it seems that a good way to deal with the 'shadow' is to undergo the antithesis, or some kind of rebellion, but this action might be done in a half-stupor, almost like when one is sleep walking."

"And so much for the wish fulfillment theory. Wishes or desires are often dictated by the 'shadow'. Be careful what you wish or it might come true, as they say. A strong wish might just lead you to commit murder as you sleepwalk. This is not to mention how the social conditions around you cooperate in the realization of your wishes, like old mothers who fell in love with Fray Antolin and unconsciously exposed their young daughters to him as workers."

"I have heard the old folks say that about Fray Antolin – the mother/daughter thing you've just said."

"I have been told that Fray Antolin was well-loved by the **Bascon** family and was always a welcome guest in their house. It would certainly have been Mrs. Bascon's idea to have her daughters work in the convent. Or, Mrs. Bascon's shadow acting out..."

"According to folklore, the older women – matrons and spinsters – would sit right under the pulpit and gaze up adoringly at the Padre as he preached. I imagine he would have been an enigmatic speaker, not to mention those eyes. Then, after each mass, these women would go to him and hand him an envelope with their contributions in it."

"That would have been the subject of scrutiny, a typical tale in history books, a leader paying the price for being popular."

"The **antithesis** seems to be the most colorful stage of the struggle. It's when you hold your breath for its entire duration and wonder whether one will ever come out of it in one piece."

"We all have our infamous versions of such tales."

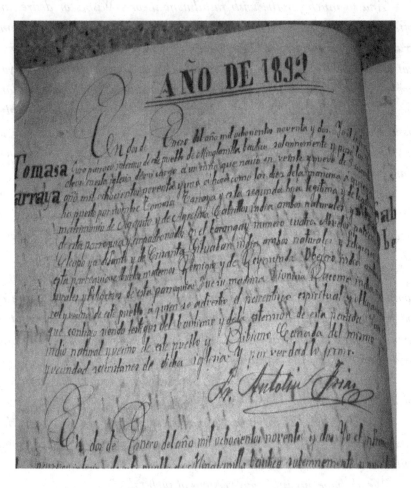

A Page from the Baptismal Records at
The Naga Parish Church. Cebu, 1892
Signed by Fr. Antolin Frias

From the private collection of the Author

**Rice lands of the former 8000-hectare Talisay-Minglanilla
Friar Estates in Cebu stretching all the way to the distant hills**

The Friar Estates

*The Talisay-Minglanilla Friar Estates covered 8,000 hectares of the
entire area of the towns of Talisay and Minglanilla during the 300
years of Spanish Colonization. It was owned by the Recoletos Order
of the Philippine Islands and was part of the 170,000 hectares of
friar lands scattered all over the Philippine colony and owned by
three Catholic orders – The Augustinians, The Recollects, and the
Dominicans.*

*In 1898 the American regime bought the friar estates of Bulacan,
Cavite, Batangas, Laguna, and Cebu, from the friar orders for
7,239,785.00 Dollars. This was known as the Friar Lands Act of
Congress of July, 1902. The lands were then apportioned for sale or lease
to the existing tenants and other interested parties under easy terms.*

**PARISH PRIEST OF SAN NICOLAS CEBU
WITH ANTOLIN FRIAS 1885-1889**

2. Rev. Fr. Casimero Herrera		1857-1859
3. Rev. Fr. Apolinar Alvarez		1859-1861
4. Rev. Fr. Pedro Hernandez		1861-1862
5. Rev. Fr. Dalmacio Cañizares		1862-1864
6. Rev. Fr. Gabriel Gonzales		1864-1865
7. Rev. Fr. Fernando Sanchez		1865-1876
8. Rev. Fr. Jorge Romanillos		1876-1877
9. Rev. Fr. Gabriel Gonzales		1877
10. Rev. Fr. Jacinto Llamas		1877-1878
11. Rev. Fr. Antonio Lastra		1878
12. Rev. Fr. Fernando Sanchez		1878-1891
13. Rev. Fr. Meliton Talegon		1891-1892
14. Rev. Fr. Luis Mayoral		1892-1893
15. Rev. Fr. Mauricio Alvarez		1893-1895
16. Rev. Fr. Valerio Rodrigo		1895-1897
17. Rev. Fr. Antolin Frias		1897-1898
18. Rev. Fr. Cayetano Bastes		1898
19. Rev. Fr. Bartolome del Carmen		1898-1914
20. Rev. Fr. Sancho Abadia		1914
21. Rev. Fr. Joaquin Boiser		1914-1933
22. Rev. Fr. Julio Fernandez		1933-1947
23. Rev. Fr. Angel Jumawan		1947-1952
24. Rev. Fr. Nicolas Navarro		1952-1953
25. Rev. Fr. Pedro Montebon		1953-1958
26. Rev. Fr. Filomeno Singson		1958-1960
27. Rev. Fr. Gregorio Montecillo		1960-1976
28. Rev. Msgr. Pablo Alcarez, H.P.		1976-1987
29. Rev. Fr. Jose Canseko		1987-1993
30. Rev. Fr. Glicerio Diosana		1993-1999
31. Rev. Msgr. Jose Montecillo, H.P.		present

PARISH PRIESTS OF ARGAO, CEBU
WITH FATHER ANTOLIN FRIAS 1897-1898

A ROSTER OF FORMER PARISH PRIESTS WITH THE
NAME OF FR. ANTOLIN FRIAS AT THE MINGLANILLA
PARISH CHURCH, CEBU

CHAPTER 7

EUSTAQUIA

I had been sitting at that table by the window in the convent since morning, engrossed on the intricate designs I was sewing on an altar cloth. I had taken only a short break for lunch and a short nap. Now the sound of crickets reminded me that it was getting late.

"Dodong, have you seen the Padre and Asay? Were they here this morning? Asay has not come home for three nights. My parents are worried." I asked the young man sitting across from me.

My sister had been spending too much time riding out to the haciendas with Padre Antolin, while I have taken over her share of the needlework.

I was overcome with hunger, but with perpetually strained eyes and a back ache, I had little energy left for cooking. Besides, all I knew to cook were chickens. I was really fed up with chickens.

"I hope the Padre comes home tonight," Dodong answered, "I can't go on cancelling the early morning masses without causing alarm. And these scheduled Baptisms on Sunday get me all nervous."

Apolonio or "Dodong" de la Cerna, the sacristan major, a man 28 years old, had been hanging around me since Padre Antolin started going out with Asay to the haciendas. One can easily imagine his tongue hanging out like a devoted dog. He would sit with me, strumming his guitar and singing one of those love songs in Binisaya, which broke my heart and made me weep. He would be delighted that he had the power to make me cry, to make me feel.

Dodong came from the neighboring barrio of San Isidro here in Talisay, where his family had been tenants in that part of the friar haciendas for generations. He had told me his story so many times, and I had been pretending to listen like I had heard it for the first time. I felt sorry for the man. Ever since he was a boy, Dodong had always wanted to be a priest. After primary school, he took tutorials in Spanish and Latin in the ciudad to prepare him for the seminary. But the young adolescent boy was simply incapable of learning the languages. He might have been good in Music or Crafts, but languages were what he needed to be a priest. He finally stopped attending school and stayed home moping in the farm. His mother finally asked the local parish priest to take him in as a sacristan. It was a welcome break. Dodong devoted himself to this sacred task happily to this day, occupying the top rank of *sacristan major*.

This was just perfect for him, since the native clergy had never been welcome in the parishes. The *peninsulares* or pure Spanish priests who were trained in Spain were hard to convince that the native secular priests could match their performance. These *creoles* or locally trained native priests, including the ones from Mexico and other colonies, were taken in as mere assistants.

"Don't you have anything to do, Dodong?" I asked. "If you are not busy, can I bother you to cook some food for both of us?"

He did not seem surprised. Lately, I had been asking him to cook our supper and he always jumped at the chance to prove himself worthy. I could feel that he was in love with me. He was just waiting for a word or gesture from me to give him a go signal. Then I was so sure he would ask me to marry him. But at that point a pet dog would get my affection more than he ever would.

[40] "*Si, Senorita*," he answered, teasing me with his Spanish.

"Ah, Dodong, you speak Spanish so well!" I giggled. My sarcasm seemed to strike a sensitive chord in this bruised young man. He looked at me with sad eyes. But then the next moment he was laughing indulgently, trying to please me.

"And Dodong, not chicken again, please. Can you get hold of some fish…or some *tapa*? I know it's late, but I'm sure that little market down the road would have them."

Dodong immediately put down his guitar to cater to my wishes. I was one lucky girl. At least there was someone who cared for me, even at my age. Dodong was far from brilliant, but he was not bad-looking. In fact, he was a *mestizo*, tall, with fair skin, light eyes, and curly hair. He also smelled good. A pleasant masculine aroma exuded from him as we sat together. I could love him for this smell, I thought, when I got really old and lonely and desperate for company. Now, to me, the most he could be was a brother. But I was almost 29 years old. I always closed my eyes when I thought of this. How long had it been since a man paid me this much attention? No one since Fernando, and that was nine years before. When I was still a juicy 20-year-old and could dance all night…

But Asay certainly had had her fair share of suitors. It was not that she was even pretty. I knew neither my sister nor I turned heads or drew whistles. Both of us were tall, with long thick wavy hair and slender build – but I at least had a larger bosom and more voluptuous hips. But what were these compared to Asay's vibrance, this charisma that I knew I lacked? Asay also rode on a horse wearing pants – such a free spirit – and she danced with such grace. But my sister had such high standards with men. I was so sure Asay would never find the man of her dreams in this little town.

Unless, of course…I dismissed the disturbing thought as quickly as it came. But I could not help but notice the change in my sister's demeanor ever since she came to work for Padre Antolin. First, I noticed that Asay had been sleeping more soundly. In our common bedroom, I knew all about the sleepless nights, the twisting and the turning. That had changed. Asay was now forever singing under her breath. With those bright eyes and purposeful movements, I saw a woman in love.

The last time I saw my sister was three days before when she and the Padre went riding off in their horses to visit the haciendas. I knew the area around Linao and how the river would just unpredictably rise, making it impassable. But there were always the little boats travelling along the shoreline. Asay and the Padre could have left their horses in good hands and returned home on one of those boats. I should not have been worried. But I was. I felt some kind of dread at the pit of my stomach.

Then I heard footsteps coming up the stairs. The door opened and I came face to face with Asay. I met my sister's eyes for a lifetime of a second, and I just knew she was not the same person she had been three days before.

Then Padre Antolin came into the room. He gave me a startled look, like he was wondering who I was.

"So you are still here, uhhh, Eustaquia…Yayang?" he finally blurted out. He even forgot my name for a moment there. "Ah, we were both stranded in the haciendas. The river suddenly rose as we were passing. We were lucky not to get washed away into the sea. We could not get through until now."

His voice sounded husky and strained.

"So you both had a little swim," I teased them. What else could I say? There was some embarassed laughter.

Then, an awkward silence.

"Oh…I sent Dodong to the little market to buy [41] *buwad* and *tapa*. About time we eat something besides chickens," I finally found my voice. "No, please don't think he and I are…you know…we were just talking, and I got hungry…"

"Oh, no such thing, Yayang. Please go ahead and help Dodong prepare the food. We are all famished," Nicolasa answered breathlessly, the lilt in her voice gone, as though she had not eaten for days.

The aroma of *buwad* frying in the stove stirred everyone's appetite, a welcome intrusion into the awkward moments before we three proceeded to the dining table.

I felt something click inside my head. A door was closing. Life for us would never be the same from now on – not for me, not for Asay, not for Padre Antolin. But I did not know that the list would include poor Dodong.

---

[40] *Yes, Miss, in Spanish*
[41] *dried salted fish, in Binisaya*

CHAPTER 8

※

PARADISE LOST

I did not see Asay again after the afternoon at the river. I was beside myself with worry. My mind kept straying back to the events of that day. I would be in the middle of delivering a sermon, then I would suddenly fall silent. And I would stare into space. The congregation must have been puzzled over my strange behavior.

Here is what really happened. Asay and I had stopped by Sidro's house on the way home.

"Just came by to tell you your children will all be home with you tonight," I told Sidro, "all three boys and the one girl who should attend to her mother. But I need the boys in the convent by Monday. [42] *Comprende*, Sidro? They will be hired to make furniture for the classrooms. We will discuss the design and the measurements there. Then they can work right here with you," I explained to Sidro as one would to a young child. He scratched his head and nodded.

"I notice you have coconut trees too old to bear any more nuts. Cut them and use them to repair your house and to make the furniture," I suggested.

"Si, Padre," Sidro answered, now smiling through his tears, [43]"*Salamat kaayo*".

On the ride back to the convento, the heat had exhausted both Asay and me, and we decided to take a rest along the riverbank. We had often done this, sitting on a grassy knoll to cool off. I would always find a tree to lean against before I dozed off. Now, after the *tuba* and the chicken, a pleasant drowsiness had crept over me. Around us, the bamboo trees creaked against the wind, lulling me to sleep.

But on this particular afternoon, the river was swollen after the rain. Deep pools had been formed between the huge stones.

"Look, Asay, look at all that water," I exclaimed like an excited boy, "I wish we could just dive in."

It took her a split second to announce, "I am going in for a swim - in these same clothes. I will surely be dry by the time we get back." And she alighted from her horse and prepared to dive in. "I'm sure you would rather nap, Padre".

I found a spot under the shade of a large bamboo tree to take my nap. I had always wanted to swim at the public beach in town – a long frustrated wish. When would I ever get the chance to do this – take a dip in cool running waters? But wait, not even here where no one was looking would it be alright for me to just dip in and swim with this young woman.

I was startled from my nap by a loud rumbling noise. Then, I heard a woman scream. Was I dreaming? The next moment I was jolted by the sight of Asay struggling towards me as the water rose over her head.

"Help! Help!" she screamed, as a wall of water rushed from upstream, carrying debris and toppling everything in its path.

A week had passed since that afternoon. Asay had not shown herself in the convento at all.

The sight of Yayang working in one corner woke me from my reverie.

"How is Asay?" I asked Yayang who had been coming for work without fail, "it has been a week since she came to work."

"Yes, I know, Padre. I too am concerned about her. She has been very quiet ever since that day. Remember that day you said you both fell into the river? She stays in bed most of the time, and my parents are starting to get worried. But then she also goes out on her horse in the afternoons and comes back way after dark. So at least it is not some physical ailment," Yayang reported.

"*Bueno*, perhaps she is just taking a much needed respite from work. Just let her be," I said, trying to appear nonchalant, although this terrible knot in my gut became tighter.

Should I have gone to the Bascon's home to seek her out? The question festered in my head for days, and I almost uttered her name out loud as I said the Mass. Finally, I convinced myself that she was a mature, intelligent woman after all, with the full capacity to make her own decisions.

"But it hurts..." I thought, as I tried in vain to sleep after each grueling day at work, "she is both the friend and the mother I've been looking for."

There were strong forces at work in the river that afternoon. Were they dark...diabolical? But how could that be? There was so much beauty there! It was all very freeing!

Then I recalled our Theology in the seminary.

"*Lucifer, although fallen, is still an angel. He can exude Beauty and Freedom. He uses it for his own dark purposes. This is where his power lies. How else ensnare you into his grasp?*" the professor had explained the paradox.

What transpired between me and Asay – I had never experienced anything more beautiful - just too overwhelming for my mind to grasp fully. There had been girls in my youth with whom I flirted around in the summers I spent at home from boarding school. But all of them were products of the traditional conservative Catholic upbringing, with mothers breathing down their backs. The strong sense of sin was ingrained in me and in all my young friends. Dirty thoughts arisen from holding a girl's hand were considered sinful and deserving of penance. The only time I got close to a girl was when we danced.

But there were the ones in my wild dreams. They seemed so real. I looked forward to these dreams, reduced to my sinful self, my animal nature in full play. What a shame!

Then, there was this woman on the same steamship with me from Spain. In each stop - Port Said, Goa, Singapore - I would alight from the ship to find her waiting for me at the dock. She was attractive, but her advances totally repulsed me, and I avoided her like a plague.

As I matured, I gradually understood the logic behind what they said was right and wrong. Mainly it was a strong, unbending dedication to the Ultimate Truth – there were clearly prescribed rules to follow – but it was all too easy to lose oneself in one's human desires and drives and stray deep into the darkness.

Or, did one have to go through Hell to rise again and be redeemed?

And what had come over me at the river? Could it be possible for one man to have more than one self – the public persona and another hiding behind it, like a shadow? Was this shadow an alternate personality formed by frustrated urges, repressed desires? Did it emerge when one was put against a corner? I was ill-prepared for such a possibility.

In the next month, I repressed all emotion and plunged myself into the tasks demanding my attention. Sidro's children had delivered the furniture for the schoolhouse and now they could start working on the repair of the classrooms. I asked Yayang and Dodong to help me set up the furniture. The two seemed to have fun working together, like two little children, but I knew their relationship lacked the flavor of anything beyond a wholesome friendship. She was obviously not in love with him.

Yayang had also shown a serious interest in teaching kids, and I thought she would make a good catechism instructor.

"If you are interested in teaching catechism, Hija, I will have to start coaching you immediately," I told her one evening, as the two of us shared one *parol* – much like I did with Asay. "Catechism instructors are badly needed now that we are preparing the children for Holy Communion next year. And don't forget there will be some adults coming in to be baptized. They will need instruction as well – of course, all in Binisaya."

"Me – teach? Padre, I would be so happy!" she exclaimed, and got up from her seat to give me a hug. I was both touched and amused at her spontaneity.

I began to look at Yayang more closely, watching for any resemblance between her and her sister, imagining that she was Asay when her back was turned.

I noticed the strong likeness between the girls when I viewed Yayang from behind, the same long dark wavy hair cascading down her back, the same grace with which she carried her head standing still. But the way her ample hips swayed when she walked was uniquely hers.

And then, there was that same voice – the same lilt – which gave me some solace.

Yayang then had to stay longer hours in the convento to catch up with catechism lessons and learn prayers in Spanish. I was happy to have one more catechist in my staff in addition to Dodong. But Yayang did not ride a horse and could not possibly get home way after dark. So I offered to give her a room in the convento right next to the servant's quarters. This seemed to be the perfect arrangement.

In the afternoons, I would meet with the town capitan to discuss improvements for the town of Talisay. Talisay had just been recently proclaimed a town, and a lot of time, energy, and expertise were needed to do the proper layout of public buildings and to appoint officials. The town plaza needed the work of an artist, and I offered the little exposure I gathered from Spain, where everyone young and old helped set up props for fiesta celebrations.

I found so much pleasure and fulfillment in this civic work. "I should have been a politician," I thought, "or a civic leader".

I felt both guilty and bewildered at the idea that I would want to be anything besides a priest. An unmistakable seed of doubt seemed to be sprouting in my heart.

One afternoon, as I rode back home in my horse, my heart gave a lurch at the sight of a woman in white riding across a corn field. Asay! It was her, with her long hair flying in the wind. I started riding as fast as I could in her direction. But as I came closer, the figure disappeared behind the bamboo trees. My mind was playing tricks, I thought, with a sinking heart.

Oh, I missed her. How I missed her!

Two months later, Señora Bascon cornered me one Sunday after mass to invite me again for lunch. I heard myself tell her that I was simply too busy. But the truth was I was just afraid. The woman seemed distraught. I could tell that she was troubled by the way she curled and uncurled her big handkerchief. Her eyes were swollen, obviously from crying.

"I have sent Asay to Bohol to live with my brother and his family," she announced in a strained voice, "perhaps Yayang has already told you that she has seemed troubled lately."

Her news hit me with a blow.

"I am very sorry to hear that, Señora Bascon. Is there anything I can do to help?" I sufficiently recovered myself to say.

She shook her head - too hard. "No, Padre, but thank you for your concern. At least we know we can count on you at any time."

That night I was roused from my sleep by a noise in the garden. I got up from bed and looked out the window at the garden below. This was one of the rare nights when a bright full moon shone through a clear sky after the rain. I saw the shadow of a woman standing in the garden below my window, her back to me. She was wearing a long white dress and her long dark hair flowed down her back in a cascade.

"Asay!" I whispered, startled by the apparition.

With my heart in my throat, I ran down to the garden to join her.

"Asay!" I called out in a soft voice. The woman turned around. It was Yayang.

"It's me, Yayang, Padre," she said with an awkward smile, "I'm sorry."

"Oh, no, Hija," I quickly answered, "I am glad it's you. You and Asay look so much alike from behind. I just came down to see why you're still here at this late hour."

"I wanted to gaze at this rare moon. When was the last time we saw the moon? Two months ago before the rain clouds covered it," she explained. "And do you smell the jasmine?"

"Yes," I said weakly, standing rooted to one spot like a statue.

Moments of silence, then she said, "You'll see her again."

⁴⁴ *"Que? Quien?"* I answered, lapsing into Spanish, disoriented. I could feel that shadow emerging from me, my other self, more like a little child drawn out by this sympathetic mother.

"Asay. Someday she will be back," she told me calmly, "I miss her, too."

I suddenly felt weak and fell on the grass, sitting there without saying a word. She remained standing.

"I had a man once," she began. "His name was Fernando. That was nine years ago and I was only twenty years old. He was a Spaniard and worked as a sailor in one of the ships travelling between Manila and Spain. I was working in the ciudad, doing needlework for the nuns. I met him at a church festival there and it was love at first sight. The relationship lasted for a month. One day he took the ship back to Spain, and never came back."

"How did you feel when he left?" I asked.

"First, I was sick with longing. I waited and I waited for a letter to come. But not a single word... Yet life goes on. I took it one day at a time. And time is a great healer. So is the miraculous Santo Niño to whom I prayed quite often," she answered calmly without a trace of emotion.

"You seem to have recovered quite well," I said.

"Padre, there is one thing I learned from that experience. It takes only one special person, and one significant experience to bring fulfillment to your entire life," the girl replied. "All else that happens seem insignificant in comparison. Let me explain. If nothing special happens to me now or ever, that month I spent with Fernando would have made my entire life – from beginning to end - worthwhile. If I had a child from that relationship, then I would not want for more."

A child – Asay – I had not thought about this!

"You sound so convinced! The experience must have been very intense," I told her.

The girl did not speak for a few moments, as though groping for the right words to express the intensity of her experience.

"Now I should go," she said, failing to find the words. "Remember, Padre, life is a precious gift. Every minute counts. Try to be happy in spite of all the pain."

I remained sitting on the grass under the full moon, inhaling the sweet aroma of jasmine. I was strangely comforted by the girls' words.

Then the next thing I remember was my servant Nardo shaking me awake. "Padre, Padre. It's almost 7 o'clock. You'll be late for your mass."

I had fallen asleep on the grass that night.

---

42 Understand? In Spanish
43 Thank you very much in Binisaya
44 What? When? In Spanish

CHAPTER 9

THE MIRACLE

Now to continue with my story. How did I survive all that? It was now October 1884 and the town of Talisay was celebrating its annual fiesta, the feast of Santa Teresa of Avila. The past months had been the most hectic for the parish, with preparations for the children's First Holy Communion, the traditional procession and the big celebration at the town square attended by the Bishop and other friars from around Cebu. There were dances, contests, banquets, among other activities. I as parish priest had been torn between my official duties and honoring so many invitations in the houses of my parishioners.

One of the dance numbers I watched was the usual *Cariñosa*, transporting me back to the time when I saw Asay dance, flitting and flirting around the stage. But the initial pangs had been reduced to an occasional twinge of sadness each time I thought of her.

After the big event, I barely had time to breathe before preparations for the Christmas season made demands on my time and energy. I plunged into my work with renewed fervor, getting up each dawn to say the *Misa de Gallo*, preparing the school children for the season presentation, honoring endless invitations, going around the haciendas to drink *tubâ* and eat *caldereta* with the tenants, working with town officials in civic matters – it was a miracle I stayed in one piece at each day's end.

Yayang had her hands full as well. There were the school Christmas program, the new repertoire for the Christmas choir, the *Belen* and the lanterns to be installed, in addition to the altar cloth she was doing for the Christmas day mass.

"*Adeste Fidelis, Laete triumphantes*," she sang with the choir, learning the Christmas hymn in Latin. The choir's rendition of the hymn was so beautiful it moved everyone to tears.

"I feel both happy and sad," she told me. "But it's a good feeling. At least you feel alive."

I agreed with her completely. There was nothing worse than to become insensitive and numb.

In the past three months, I had been sending Yayang and Dodong regularly to the Cebu Cathedral in the ciudad to have voice lessons with a Spanish music instructor. I wanted them to learn the latin *Ave Maria* by Bach-Gounod so they would be able to sing it for the midnight mass on Christmas Eve. This was my mother, Luisa's, favorite. I knew I was too ambitious – it took many years of training and extraordinary talent for anyone to be able to cope with this demanding piece of work. But I was hoping for a miracle.

Yayang seemed enthralled by the hymn and the Latin sounds. She seemed to be walking on air those days, in love with life itself. But with little training, she could not cope with the high notes. To everyone's surprise, Dodong's voice range was perfect for the hymn. More surprising was the easy way with which Dodong managed the Latin sounds. I arranged for Yayang to sing the lower notes and Dodong to take over with the high notes. With the help of a church organist sent from the Cebu Cathedral, the performance turned out a raving success. Their voices reverberated around the huge church, causing not a few conversions. From then on, the pair had been asked to perform at weddings and funerals.

"*Ave Maria, Gratia Plena...*" Yayang went, a delicate note of sadness in her voice. She was surely thinking of her sister Asay.

She did not yet know that very soon she would need to pray very hard for herself as well.

"We have been sent a miracle, Hija," I told Yayang, "only a miracle would enable an untrained singer to sing the Ave Maria." And as usual she simply gave me an affectionate hug.

"And, Padre, listen to all that Latin coming from Dodong's lips," Yayang laughed, "only a miracle would enable Dodong to produce those sounds, and so beautifully."

"I felt a host of angels singing through you and Dodong," I said. "I have been praying for a miracle as a sign of God's mercy. Now, we have been granted one – with you as instruments," I pointed out to this ecstatic young woman.

This particular incident made me feel the depth of God's love and the extent of his forgiveness. After months of inner turmoil since the day at the river, I finally felt a deep peace.

The chill in the air aroused the familiar feeling of nostalgia in everyone. I felt homesick for my family and my hometown. I wished I were with my aging father, my sister and her children, the older folk and the people in our village. Christmas was one of the rare times I would go home from boarding school and later from the seminary. There was so much eating, laughing and crying. Wrapped in woolen blankets, family and friends would share a warm drink in front of a cozy fireplace while icicles formed in the window panes.

But this life in the town of Talisay was the life I chose, here in this "camp". Christmas just made it a little harder to bear.

Dodong and Yayang have made it a lot easier, though. The two had proven themselves indispensable in the parish and the school. Their simplicity and lighthearted disposition had lightened my burden.

I also had a gift for each of them. I gave Dodong a green felt hat with a brown and white feather. I had brought it with me from Spain as a memento of my trips to the mountains with my parents.

"Dodong, this hat holds many special memories. I have given it to you because you too are special," I proclaimed.

And I gave Yayang a rare tortoise shell comb. "Yayang, this comb belonged to my mother. She would put it on her coiffured hair on special occasions, at Christmas, on her birthday, when she danced the *flamenco*".

Yayang was overwhelmed. She gave me yet again a spontaneous peck in the forehead, evoking laughter all around us.

"She has the spirit of a little child – so innocent and simple," I thought.

In return Yayang gave me a black knitted sweater. "My mother and I made this ourselves, Padre. We thought of you with each stitch," the solemnity in her face almost made me laugh. Instead, I gave her a warm smile.

"Oh, thank you so much, Yayang. They say the best gifts are those you make with your own hands".

I also wished that Yayang's gift was anything but a black color.

CHAPTER 10

THE CATHARSIS

The season came and went. Then the weeks flew by into April and the summer season. School had finally ended for the summer break. Farmers had finished harvesting their crops and were sitting back idly in the heat, waiting for the next planting season in June when the rains would come.

But I could not look forward to any real vacation – I, Padre Antolin, parish priest and administrator of the haciendas, had to stay in my post the year round. At least, I did not have to teach school. This was the time of the year when everyone around the islands indulged their indolence and enjoyed preparations for the town fiestas.

Yayang had asked permission to take a short leave. She was leaving for Bohol with her parents. I knew they were going to visit Asay.

"Is there any problem?" I asked her.

"No, we're just taking a short summer break," Yayang replied. "I will be back in a week's time, Padre." But she seemed evasive and kept her eyes downcast.

But I was not easily fooled. My intuition told me the Bascons had a problem. Yayang's demeanor said it all.

Then, a thought hit me. I almost toppled over from its impact. "Is it possible…that Asay went away to have a baby?" I asked myself. It was not unusual in a small community such as Talisay for young unmarried women to hide their pregnant condition by leaving home and having their baby elsewhere.

"Where is she?" I wondered desperately. "She might not even be in Bohol. She might just be in the ciudad right here in Cebu."

I resisted the strong impulse to take my horse and ride away as far as I could - to a place where I could forget who I was and make a fresh start.

[45] "*Miserere nobis, Miserere nobis...*" I implored.

That night I did get my wish – to run away so far that I would forget all that had happened. But I did not need my horse to get there. I was in a kind of limbo. I had preached about limbo many times before that, and this time I knew what it really was. I was everywhere and nowhere at the same time.

In this never-never-land, I finally got my long frustrated wish – to swim in the ocean. But this time it was a river. It flowed around me swiftly. I could feel the strong currents massage my body. Then I realized I was totally naked. But I was not ashamed. I was enjoying every minute of it.

There was someone there with me. Another body was splashing around me. Then, I saw that it was Asay. She was just waist-deep into the water and her long dark hair covered her bare breasts. Venus rising!

She was looking at me with her lips parted – that same hungry look which for me meant danger. But she was different than all the rest. I reached out to her. Then, everything went dark.

Then my mother was there, looking quite radiant in her wide-brimmed straw hat. She sat in the middle of a sunlit field. Her face blended with the sunflowers, huge golden blooms dancing with the wind.

[46]"*Ven aqui!*" she called out to me, "Antolin, *Hijo....*"

I walked in her direction, but suddenly a huge snake reared its ugly head and hissed right into my face.

Dimly, like from a great distance, I heard incantations. I could smell the smoke of incense and burning flesh. Walls alternately closed in and receded around me. And always there were the snakes, coiling and hissing around my head.

Then, I opened my eyes and saw someone peering at my face. It was Dodong. His eyes were very sad, with dark circles around them.

"Padre...padre!" he almost screamed with joy. "You're awake! I thought you would never wake up."

"Padre, you had a fever for many days," he proceeded to explain, "You were delirious and mumbling in your sleep. I have been here all the time praying hard for you."

Dodong had made a makeshift bed outside my bedroom. My dim awareness of his presence was reassuring as I muttered away into the night.

While I was sick, the servants had taken it upon themselves to call an [47]*albulario*, a bent old woman who came with a paraphernalia of weird objects – roots, oils, dried bones of unknown origin - and I remembered the vague smell of burning flesh and the sound of incantations as I lay feverish.

"Ahhh...it's that old wound," they told me what the old magician said, shaking her head with a long sigh, "a gaping wound in his spirit. It's very old, very old..."

"I thought you had the St. Anthony's Fire – *El fuero de San Antonio* - which infected the pilgrims along the Camino de Santiago in Spain," Dodong said, "Remember you told me about this? It was also called 'the devil's sickness', the devil's ploy to waylay the pilgrims from their holy mission."

The ones afflicted by this disease suffered from madness. Their limbs became gangrenous and fell off one after the other. In my hometown, Castrogeriz, still stands the building of the old hospital and monastery of the Order of St. Anthony where the pilgrims were treated for the sickness. Was the same devil driving me mad – to waylay me from my sacred mission – like he did those pilgrims?

I felt Dodong praying very hard. The purity of his soul would conquer the demons. I started to feel a ray of hope. Then, Dodong started playing his guitar in my bedside, old folk songs in Binisaya, a heart pining for some lost love. And I knew I was not alone.

In between songs, he would tell me tales from his boyhood, about a stupid donkey named Pedrito, pitted against a smart stallion, Pablo. They were so funny that I finally laughed. Each burst of laughter healed me bit by bit. And the fever finally abated.

"I have asked to be assigned away from here, Dodong," I told my hero right after I recovered from my mysterious ailment. "In a few months, I will be at the San Nicolas Parish."

Dodong looked startled. Then, he bowed his head and started to cry. I put an arm around his shoulder. The two of us men – unshaven and unwashed – hugged each other tight.

"Stop that, Dodong. You remind me of the little lost lamb I found when I was a boy. It kept on bleating far into the night for its mother. One never forgets such a sound – an infant crying out for its mother. At one time or the other, each one of us – you and I – no matter how old, cry out for our mother," I said.

"You will still be working for the Talisay parish. You are needed here. I can promise you that," I added. "And look, I will still be ultimately in charge of Talisay Parish as well as the Haciendas. You and I will be seeing each other regularly on my visits."

"So what happened to the little lost lamb?" Dodong asked like a child.

"It died. That's how important mothers are," I answered.

"That's how important a good woman is," Dodong replied with innate wisdom.

---

[45] *have mercy on us, in Latin*
[46] *come here…son, in Spanish*
[47] *Medicine man*

CHAPTER 11

UTTER DEVOTION

I was back from Bohol and given the task of helping the Padre pack his belongings for his new assignment. I was finally admitted into his bedroom with the task of putting his personal effects in huge chests. I would sit there for a long while, idly, just savoring the surrounding magic. I would gaze for long periods at the sturdy *narra* bed with just a mat instead of a mattress and the pillowcases of exquisitely embroidered linen. I would inhale the aroma of camphor. In another corner I would run my fingers across the smooth surface of the mahogany chest. The mysterious brown and black stripes of the [48]*kamagong* desk told its own story, its top littered with lots of pens and stationery.

But what amazed me were the books. I had never seen so many books in one place – books on the shelves, on the floor, under the bed, piled high on top of the desk.

All that those books would bring into the life of a man - what more could he want? How much richer my life would have been if only I could read all these books!

But all we girls were taught in school were the very basic Reading and Arithmetic and lots of religion and homemaking skills, like cooking and sewing.

So, here I was, in this room, basking in its glory. I felt like the walls were a womb, enclosing me for an eventual rebirth. I just knew I would emerge from this experience a different person.

Little did I suspect that my wish would soon come true – and with so much birth pains.

Waking from my reverie, I would start packing up the Padre's things. But when I opened the drawers containing his clothes, a familiar aroma assailed me. I felt like I was digging my nose into Padre Antolin's chest, inhaling the raw sweat. My knees gave way, and I sat on the floor for an hour and wept.

Padre Antolin had been everything to me – a mentor, a spiritual guide, a friend, the brother I never had. Nobody had ever trusted me so utterly. He made me believe in myself. I would miss the lessons most of all. He had been the only real teacher I ever had. Without him, what would life be like - for myself as well as for many people in all of Talisay?

A pall had descended on the town as news of Padre Antolin's transfer spread.

"*Ay*, Yayang," Dodong said to me with a deep sigh, "these matrons and young women who adore Padre Antolin from below the pulpit – what are they going to do now?"

"And the contributions to the church," I joked, "that would suffer most of all. I hope the next parish priest would have the same enigmatic personality – those magnetic eyes – the powerful voice..."

"And the warm generous nature," Dodong added.

"You have been very quiet these days, Yayang," Dodong told me as we ate lunch. "Something besides Padre Antolin's departure is bothering you. I can feel it. So, what's all the mystery?"

I groped for words.

"So how is Asay?" he prodded me on. "And how was your trip to Bohol? Come on, you can cry on these shoulders." He gave a little pat on his shoulder.

I finally burst into violent sobs, holding on to Dodong's arm for support. After a few minutes, I calmed down sufficiently to talk to him.

"Dodong, I trust you to keep this to yourself. Asay had a baby girl last April. Everything went well for the mother and child. But, Dodong, you should have seen all that pain, all that blood. Oh, Dodong, having a baby can really tear a woman's body apart," I whimpered.

Dodong did not seem surprised. He simply became very quiet, as though deep in thought.

"But, Yayang," he finally spoke, clasping my hands in his own, "how did Asay take it all?"

"Oh," I said, feeling my spirits lifting at the thought of Asay. "Asay was ecstatic. She had this blissful look on her face, like someone deeply fulfilled. I just felt this child was what she had been waiting for all her life."

"Then, why those tears, as though your world was ending?" Dodong asked. "Asay is happy about the baby. That's all that matters, isn't it?"

I lapsed into a confused silence.

"Oh, I understand," Dodong continued, giving me a brilliant smile, as though life were one big joke, "it seems to me you feel left out, Yayang. You feel you have lost your sister. Not only that but you are anxious if you will ever have your own child."

All I could do was nod a little. I found that I could tell Dodong everything and he would remain a loyal friend.

"That day will soon come," Dodong consoled me. "It won't be long before you will have your own child. I have a feeling you will have a son."

I laughed and gave the man a little shove.

"We don't know who the father of the baby is," I said after our little skirmish, "Asay simply refused to tell us how it happened."

"I feel you know more than you are telling me, Yayang," he told me like a brother. "So, anyway, tell me about the baby."

"It's a beautiful baby girl," I told him. "She has thick, black hair - very curly. By a sunny window you can see that her eyes are very light, almost green."

"Her name is Fidelina."

---

[48] *Black hardwood with brown strips*

CHAPTER 12

THE SECOND CHILD

It has been three months since I left Talisay and occupied my post as parish priest of San Nicolas de Tolentino Parish, a short distance from the Ciudad de Cebu.

The new assignment turned out to demand less of my energy. Here in this heavily populated city parish, there were other priests to assist me.

But I found this bustling commercial district near the Ciudad too frenetic for my taste. The smell of fish emanating from the fish market for miles around had deprived me of sleep in the nights after a busy market day, when the fishermen brought in their catch from the town's shore.

Since 1565, the town of San Nicolas had been occupied by the Indios - the indigenous native population - a community segregated from the Ciudad where only the Spaniards and the mestizos lived. The town's ambience was consequently more humble and less pretentious than the more affluent neighborhoods in the Ciudad.

I longed for the quiet and serenity of Talisay, for the pure air around the rice fields, the sound of birdsong at sunset, of the Magtalisay trees swaying in the wind, of rivers flowing. I wished I could take my horse out into the horizon in the large friar haciendas there. I missed the sound of silence.

I missed the people, especially the ones closest to me. But I could not bring myself to visit the folks in Talisay just yet. I was not sure I had recovered from the pain which compelled me to leave the town. So I went to Talisay only for brief inspection tours.

So, I busied myself with the management of the two parishes. I had plenty of social calls to make among the families here, starting with the houses of the government officials and going down the hierarchy. I also had to honor the frequent invitations of my fellow Agustinians for meriendas and chats at the nearby Sto. Niño Church.

As though these activities were not demanding enough, the Augustinian Order had put me in charge of the archives of the Cebu province. The books and records there had been in complete disarray, and putting things in order was a gargantuan task. There were volumes of the *Revistas Agustiniana*'s to compile; books, journals, periodicals to catalog; legal documents to classify – all scattered around the library of the Santo Niño Church.

But I want to tell you of that day – when my life took another turning point. I was scheduled to have lunch with the Barrio Capitan to plan the coming fiesta, merienda with the bishop to discuss countless matters, a meeting with a ladies' sewing club to inspect the new vestments. I came back to the convento around 9 in the evening. As I entered the parlor, I was surprised to see a man sleeping in one of the cushioned seats. The next instant, I realized it was Dodong.

A male servant came and whispered to me that this man, referring to Dodong, had been waiting for me since early afternoon. No words would convince him to come back another time. I asked the servant to bring him a glass of water.

I shook Dodong a little. He gave a start and, seeing me, immediately tried to compose himself.

"Dodong, it's perfectly alright. You can relax. Here have some water," I said.

Dodong sat up, rubbing his eyes, and mumbled his thanks for the water.

"Have you had something to eat, Dodong?" I asked gently, my hand on his shoulder.

Met with silence from Dodong, I ordered my servant to lay out the table with some food. But Dodong refused to eat. I finally convinced him to take some bananas while we both sat at the table. I was famished.

"Yayang is pregnant!" Dodong broke the news as I ate my dinner.

I almost choked the wine. The air around us crackled. I felt my face and neck turning crimson. I sat back and crossed my arms to hide my trembling hands in the folds of my sleeve.

Dodong looked surprised at my obvious distress. "Don't worry, Padre. I'm going to marry her as soon as possible," he declared.

"Are you the baby's father?" I finally found my voice.

"Ah, Padre, does it matter? I love Yayang. That's the only thing that matters to me," the man answered, very sure of himself.

"But what about her? Does she love you, Dodong?" I asked him very gently. "Dodong, can you imagine being married to a woman who does not love you? Do you realize how much you have to give of yourself in a good marriage? Will you not someday resent the child who is not yours? I do not want you to be miserable all your life. You are like a brother to me."

"Padre, I am going to take that risk. I pray Yayang will learn to love me. It will only take some time. I will work on it," the man answered with burning fervor in his voice. "She will learn to love me in the end."

That's what they all said – in the beginning. We sat together in silence for a few minutes, absorbed in our own thoughts.

"I came here to ask you – will you officiate at our wedding?" Dodong asked.

Stunned silence. Then I shook my head sadly. "Ah, Dodong, I am terribly sorry. I am just too busy right now. Many important matters need my undivided attention all at once," I said.

Dodong looked like he was about to cry. But he soon composed himself, and holding his head high, he said he understood perfectly.

What a big hero Dodong was! I, a priest, could never be that noble.

"But, Dodong, please don't forget this. Anytime you need anything, like money or work, please don't hesitate to come to me. I am always here to help you," I added.

Little comfort for such huge damage!

"So, Padre, thank you for your time. I have to be heading home now," Dodong took his leave. We hugged before he left.

"Dodong, wait!" I called out as he walked away, "If the baby is a boy, could you name him Jose?"

Dodong did not say a word. He stayed rooted by the door,

"When I was ten, my mother died giving birth to twins. The boy died at birth, but the girl, Olimpia, survived," I explained. "We baptized the boy Jose."

Dodong could only nod weakly. Then he said, "Of course, Padre. Jose sounds like a nice name for a boy. I promise you we will give him your dead brother's name."

When he left, I sat back and could not eat another morsel. Was this the moment when I should take a whip and flagellate myself?

CHURCH OF SAN NICOLAS PARISH, CEBU – 18th century -
A portrait in the wall of the San Nicolas Parish Rectory, Cebu City
(Courtesy of the Parish of San Nicolas, City of Cebu)

MAIN ALTAR OF SAN NICOLAS PARISH CHURCH - 2017

THE PARISH OF SAN NICOLAS DE TOLENTINO: *The present building has replaced the old one which was built in 1787. The Parish of San Nicolas de Tolentino was established in the year 1584. The parish was extended into "visitas" or chapels around the province of Cebu. Gradually, the visitas themselves, like Talisay, Pardo, Naga, and Opon, were declared as parishes themselves. The church was made of rubble-work, 67 meters long, 17 meters wide, and 19 meters high. In those days, churches were constructed according to an ancient arrangement in which the faithful worked voluntarily without pay. The people in the town supported the workers with contributions of food and money. San Nicolas, just 1.5 km from the center of the ciudad, originated from a settlement called San Miguel, as Miguel Lopez de Legaspi named it in 1565. In the 1600's it was populated by the Indios, as the native population was classified during the Spanish regime. It was in this direction that the Indios were driven away from the other districts which were occupied by Spaniards, Spanish mestizos, and Spanish-Chinese mestizos or Sangley. In this town closed to the seashore, the Indios engaged in fishing, farming, and trade. San Nicolas is presently a bustling commercial district in the City of Cebu, with a large fish market.*

CHAPTER 13

APOLONIO, THE HEROIC LAYMAN

I always thought of myself as an ordinary man, with simple needs. It took so little to make me happy, so I always slept peacefully into the night, content with just being alive.

That I had longed to be a priest is an old story. Obviously, I was not gifted enough to be one, but since Padre Antolin took me in as sacristan, I knew it was the life for me. I did not want anything more than this. Immersing myself in church rituals, the smell of incense, the Gregorian chant, the aura of devotion, teaching Catechism – what more could I want?

Little did I know so much more would be asked of me. Not until that fateful night when I went to see Padre Antolin. Not until I was faced with Yayang's pregnant condition.

After my talk with the Padre, it was so late that I was lucky to find a [49] tartanilla at the market to take me back to Talisay. I was hungry and tired. The horse's gallop soon lulled me to sleep in the back seat of the carriage.

Then I was jolted awake by a disturbing thought. It was something that Padre Antolin said – what was it? Some unspoken message I had missed… With only a few bananas in my stomach and my head still a bit fuzzy, I was too confused to pinpoint it.

Why did the padre look so upset at the news about Yayang? One would think it was his responsibility. But he is close to her family. Why would he not be concerned? Especially after Asay ran away...

But why would the padre want the baby named after his dead brother, Jose?

The answer gradually seeped through my stupor. I crossed my arms against my chest, as though recoiling from a violent blow.

Was it the time Yayang spent so much time in the Padre's bedroom, packing up his things? I recalled how upset Yayang had been at the time, what with Asay's situation and the Padre's transfer? A terrible personal crisis had caught both the Padre and the young woman together in a whirlpool of confusion.

"Stop, stop!" I shouted at the [50] *cochero*. "I want to get off here."

"But we are still in Pardo. Talisay is still about half an hour away," he said, astonished.

"It's fine, I am going to run the rest of the way," I answered without thinking.

"What? It's almost midnight," the *cochero* said, incredulous. [51] "*Sige, bahala ka.*"

I jogged slowly towards Talisay. The road was dark but a large full moon and a host of stars guided me along the way. The strong wind against my face slowly cleared my head. It must have been way past midnight when I reached Talisay. I found myself at the beach, my shoes buried in the sand. I did not know how I got there. The bright moon left a path in the still waters. The sea air soothed and comforted me.

Nature had contrived to provide solace to me - a distraught young man. I gathered some dead coconut leaves and lay down under one of the Magtalisay trees.

"What matters is that I will have Yayang by my side for the rest of our lives together," I talked to myself in the surrounding darkness. "It does not matter now if Padre Antolin is the baby's father. I love the man. He has made me who I am — a brave and dignified person."

"I will have a handsome and talented baby boy named Jose," I finally said to myself before falling into a deep sleep.

The following morning, with the sun shining brighter for me than ever before, I eagerly waited at the convento for Yayang to come to work.

"I went to see Padre Antolin last night," I told her, holding my breath for her response.

She was quiet, too quiet. "What did you tell him?" she finally found her voice.

"I asked him to officiate at our wedding," I said.

"Our wedding? Are you mad, Dodong? I will certainly not marry you. I and my child will only make you miserable all your life. I can't do that to any man, especially someone as nice as you," she said, aghast at my words.

"Yayang, think of your family - your mother. Are you sure you can dump this on her, after what happened to Asay? Think, Yayang. Here I am, a man who loves you – to eternity. I will consider myself fulfilled – just serving you all our lives," I implored.

"What did Padre Antolin say?" she asked, her voice tight with emotion.

"He said he can't come for the wedding. But, if there is anything we need, like money or work, I can approach him any time," I answered, watching Yayang closely.

Yayang sat still, too still, her eyes downcast. Around us the world quivered.

"And Yayang, please don't be afraid. I won't even touch you if you don't want me to. We could even sleep apart – in different rooms if you want, Yayang", I assured her, my voice tremulous with unshed tears.

"What? Dodong, I could not do that to you. You – just a normal young man with needs…" she protested.

"Yayang, you must not forget that once I wanted so badly to be a priest. I can sublimate my own personal needs for a higher cause," I said, sounding very resolute.

My sobriety seemed to strike a strange chord in Yayang. She finally broke into hysterical laughter. To her, it all seemed so absurd, so hilarious! I thought it was quite scary, and yet so touching…

"Okay, Dodong. I will marry you," Yayang announced.

Then she started singing the *Ave Maria* in a very mocking manner. I stood rooted to one spot, scared.

"*Ave Maria...Gratia Plena...Dominus Tecum...*"

Still laughing and singing the sacred hymn, she got up from her chair and danced slowly into her quarters.

"Yayang, wait. Padre Antolin also told me to name the baby Jose," I shouted after her, "after his dead brother".

She paused, but only for a second. Then, she flew fast to her room in another wing, and the loud slam of the door echoed through the house.

I could imagine Yayang fallling into her bed, weeping. She did not leave her room the entire day. I stood by her door and heard her weeping far into the night.

As the first rooster crowed at break of dawn, she finally fell silent, and I knew she had fallen into a deep sleep. In the morning a bright sun from the window would wake her, its warmth enveloping her like an embrace. The sad events of the last few months would seem to have happened in another world, another time. They will have lost their power to destroy her.

She would simply be filled with joy at the thought of having a handsome and talented baby boy named Jose.

I was very sure of this. She and I were kindred souls.

---

49 *a horse-drawn carriage, in Binisaya*

50 *coachman, in Binisaya*

51 *Okay, it's up to you, in Binisaya*

"Great men stand outside of morality as being ahead of their time, thus no moral claims are made on them. So great a figure must crush many an innocent flower in its path as he stands outside of virtues and pursue only the Universal".

"Nothing is lost or destroyed but raised up and preserved as in a spiral."

- You-tube THUS SPOKE MITCH Nov. 26, 2013 "Hegel's Philosophy of Freedom"

DISCUSSION IV
The Women

"I did not know Hegel could be so bohemian", I told M in one of our intellectual discussions. "I think I can use this quote in my story. Antolin Frias was not exactly a great man, but he was certainly a man of position in the community. He was expected to be no less than perfect".

"Well, he had to make some difficult moral choices," M. replied. "And in his position, he was not left with so many options. I guess he was just too important to the community. Things would have fallen apart had he left it."

"His personal life – or rather his emotional life - would have to have been set aside for the general welfare."

My cousins and I were gathered around the room to celebrate our aunt **Tia Nic's (Nicolasa Regner Lazo)** 86th birthday party. Tia Nic is the the last surviving grandchild of Fray Antolin and **Nicolasa Bascon** through our grandmother, **Fidelina Bascon Regner**.

The conversation soon turned around the book I planned to write on Fray Antolin. We were savoring the crispy [52] lechon, pancit, lumpia, and the huge chocolate birthday cake in the Lazo family's resthouse by the side of a large creek, surrounded by large mango trees. The continuous chirping and shrieking of birds lent magic to the air. The romantic atmosphere was conducive for travelling back in time to discuss our ancestors.

"Obviously, **Lola Asay** had our grandmother, Fidelina, on her own with the help of her folks. She must have been an extraordinary woman to have borne her child and bring it up on her own."

"It is easy to believe that the Bascon family was independent and decent enough not to make a fuss over paternity issues. Lola Asay might not even have told anyone who the father of her child was. This is just what my intuition tells me. I want to believe she was that kind of woman. So considerate and brave..."

"And dignified, considering the circumstances she was in. Just like you and you and you..." a male cousin pointed to the ladies around.

"Me?" one of the women protested, "I'm still a virgin." Everyone enjoyed one big hearty laugh. Just then a large bird gave a loud shriek. We all laughed louder.

"I was told that Lola Asay was not so young anymore when they met. Most likely, Frias and she were the same age, 25, or she might even have been older by a year or two. In those days, 25 was a spinster. She certainly was not one of those immature giggly adolescents prone to abuse by older men."

"She knew what she was doing, alright. But, how did she look? Was she pretty?"

"She had Malayan features, but she was fair-skinned. And she was tall, with a nice figure. This is what I've been told by the old folks. My intuition tells me her appeal lay in her character. If you analyze her life story, you would feel the same way I do – she was a real survivor to the end of her long life."

"The kind of woman who rode a horse, and danced on stage, as well?"

"And still had a man even in her advanced years. Tia Ceding told me his name was **Sanchez**, yet she does not carry that name in her tombstone," I told them what our aunt, **Ms. Praxedes Mancao Regner**, had generously shared of what she knew about Lola Asay.

"We must review our belief that the women of the past centuries were wimps and that all the men were chauvinists. A closer look at their lives would catch up by surprise."

"People walked out of each other's lives a lot in those days. Travel was difficult and inefficient. There were no cars. Now, we have the jets. That *makes long distance relationships possible. In those times, when someone left you, it was goodbye. You're lucky if that person would be able to come your way again."*

"Also, think of the mail, of how long it took to get a message across. Wasn't it terrible? Now, we have the e-mail, the facebook, the balikbayan box – everything it takes to bridge the distance."

"So, one had to be brave enough to remain in one piece after goodbyes had been said," we all agreed.

"And console oneself with a mindset – that one significant person and event makes his entire life worthwhile."

"That mindset seems a bit too drastic and risky as well. One just can't jump into a relationship and not think of consequences. Irresponsible, isn't it? But getting involved with another human being, unpredictable as most humans are, always carries with it a risk. Nothing and no one lasts forever. We all have to learn to let go…graciously."

"As the Buddhists expound on this point so well – live in the present with no attachment to the outcome. At least, this is what my limited understanding tells me," someone said.

*"Okay, well said, all of you. Everyone here deserves a Nobel prize. By the way, correct me if I'm wrong, but weren't there two Bascon sisters working in the convent – **Nicolasa** and the other with a really unique name – was it Eustaquia?"*

*"Oh yes, I have often wondered about that one. It seems really weird, but someone told me years ago that **Eustaquia** also had a child by Padre Antolin," I said.*

"According to folklore, Nicolasa had a child before her sister, Eustaquia. I have been searching the records, and I have not found anything official to prove the exact relationship between the two women. In Talisay the surname Bascon is so common that the two girls might even be just cousins," someone wondered.

*"No, they were really sisters," I told them. "There has simply been so much belief about this relationship for generations, that we don't need any documents to prove it. According to folklore, the 'sacristan major', **Apolonio de la Cerna**, was intimidated into marrying the pregnant Eustaquia. But*

my intuition tells me that he was in love with her and saw the opportunity to marry her when she got pregnant. The son, **Jose,** *married and had children,* **Isidra** *and* **Juanita.** *Jose has two living granddaughters –* **Alma Lastimosa** *and* **Lucy Mercado** *- now both residing in Talisay. And these beautiful women were kind enough to provide me with information about Eustaquia and Apolonio de la Cerna."*

"I went all the way to Pook, Talisay to see Ms. Lastimosa," I went on. "The moment I saw her, I was struck by her beauty. She looks quite the Spanish mestiza and youthful for someone over sixty. Her young grandson, **Krambikov,** *was there, and he was quite eager to provide us with information about the family tree. He told us that Eustaquia was very good at needlework. Clearly, she was needed in the parish to make vestments. She also sang in the choir," I went on. "We thank Kram so much for this precious information."*

"Nicolasa or Lola Asay and Eustaquia both worked in the convento. From stories, we make an educated guess that the mother Bascon encouraged this. The two sisters were no longer very young – perhaps in their mid or late twenties. Then Lola Asay had Padre Frias's child – Lola Peding – and then Eustaquia had his child - Lolo Jose," someone elaborated.

"Then, **Krambikov** *went on to say that the sacristan,* **Apolonio de la Cerna,** *offered to marry* **Eustaquia** *when she got pregnant with Lolo Jose. So,* **Lolo Jose** *was born with surname de la Cerna," I said further, while everyone at the dinner table listened, fascinated by the story.*

"My God! So, how did Eustaquia and her husband get along? Did they live happily ever after?" someone asked.

"Apparently, since they had many more children of their own – namely **Carmen de la Cerna Belleza, Pastor de la Cerna, Rita, Presentacion,** *and triplets who died in childbirth. The Bellezas and other descendants still live in Talisay up to now.* **Pastor,** *incidentally, had a high rank in government. He was Provincial Treasurer of Bukidnon and then treasurer of Tacloban and Davao," I answered,* **"Melchora Belleza,** *Carmen's daughter, was kind enough to provide me with this information."*

"Lola Peding and Jose de la Cerna, believed to be her half-brother, were quite close. He came to see her often."

"I knew Lolo Jose. He often came to the house to see Papa when I was a little boy. He was forever wearing a green hat with a narrow brim," my brother Boy shared.

"He came to see us, too. And he was always with Lola Peding on Sundays. They had a meal together. There was always a place for him in her table," Lilia contributed.

"Mercifully for him, Padre Antolin had his hands overflowing with work to dwell on his private torments. With the burden of his mission, would he still have the time or energy for his emotional needs?" someone asked.

We all fell silent for a minute, our mouths busy munching [53] pinaypay and sikwate, old Talisay favorites of our childhood.

"Why would a man not leave the priesthood to marry the woman he loved, especially if she was going to have his child?" the question came up.

"To pursue a sacred mission, like the priesthood, one must cast aside all else. The great **Fr. Andres Urdaneta** also had a daughter with a native woman while in the Moluccas. He was not yet a priest then but one of the trusted young sailors on the Loaisa expedition. This was prior to the Magellan expedition. He took both mother and child back to Spain with him and settled them in Portugal. Then, he went on with his life, became a priest, and came to colonize the Philippines with **Miguel Lopez de Legaspi**, leaving his daughter in Europe. That certainly would have caused him pain. But the mission he had to do for God and humanity loomed larger than any other tasks."

"So what about any emotional or psychological trauma on both woman and child?" someone asked.

"That's the inevitable question and one not easy to answer," I replied. "Each case is unique and goes a lot deeper than the surface. The woman who is of legal age is just as responsible as the man for entering into a relationship and facing its consequences. But on our own, we can't grasp fully another man's battle - against God, against nature, against other men, or against himself. In time, as the larger scheme unfolds, things fall into place. Then we stop thinking of ourselves as victims, and are healed."

"All's well that ends well'," as Shakespeare points out," I added. "There certainly is a sacred purpose in the birth of a child, though the circumstances surrounding its birth may not seem ideal. But this purpose becomes evident only when the child is grown, and at this point the sad events surrounding its birth seem moot and unimportant."

"Blessed be the woman who knows her place in the life of a great man with a larger mission to fulfill than to be her husband."

"So, you see just how resilient we all are? It runs in the family..."

"But in the end all this interpretation of past events would be educated guesses..."

"Ice cream, anyone?" came the welcome invitation.

---

[52] a whole pig roasted in open fire, noodles, native dumplings, in Binisaya
[53] fried bananas cut and shaped like a fan; a drink made of pure cocoa, in Binisaya

FIDELINA BASCON REGNER (1885-1954) AND
LOSELO D. REGNER

Fidelina was the daughter of Fr. Antolin Frias
and Nicolasa Bascon

Luis
1909-1999

Rafaela
1917-1996

Elpidia
1914-1982

Sebastian
1920-1986

Antolin
1912-1939

Leo
1922-1969

Lorenzo
1924-2005

Andrea
1926-2012

Nicolasa
1928-2015

Dionisio
1930-1981

Children of
Loselo Regner and Fidelina Bascon Regner

Author **EVELYN REGNER SENO** with grandmother
FIDELINA BASCON REGNER in Talisay, Cebu - 1952

BASCON-REGNER FAMILY REUNION
Top Row L-R: **Lino, Sebastian, Emmanuel, (5 guests), Evelyn, Elda**
Lower R: **Lorenzo, Mary Ann, Lourdes, Leo, Lito, Willy, Mario, Joy**
(1960)

CAPT. SEBASTIAN BASCON REGNER, grandson of
Antolin Frias and Nicolasa Bascon (Author's Father)
(1946)

ELPIDIA REGNER ARQUILLANO, (1914-1984)
granddaughter of ANTOLIN FRIAS and NICOLASA
BASCON (photo courtesy of Lilia Arquillano Abellanosa)

Rafaela Regner Du with children Romeo
Banjamin, and Demosthenes

Juanita de la Cerna Mercado,
daughter of Jose de la Cerna,
son of Fr. Antolin Frias and
Eustaquia Bascon

2015

L to R - Alma Lastimosa and Lucy Cañares, children of Juanita de la Cerna Mercado
and grandchildren of Jose Bascon de la Cerna

From the private collection of the Author

CHAPTER 14

SUNRISE IN NAGA

The next year 1887 found me commuting in my carriage between San Nicolas and Talisay, taking charge of both parishes as well as the Haciendas de Talisay. With the help of priests from Mexico and South America to do the minor tasks, my load got lighter. These priests were popularly known as *creoles* as compared to priests from Spain, the *peninsulares*.

But the *creoles* priests themselves had problems unique to their background and training, or the lack of it. There had been reports of misconduct, some of which involved women, drunkenness, mishandling of funds, among others. These had presented an added challenge to us parish priests.

My natural talent for advocacy served me well in these times. A skill, polished in years of settling disputes between tenant and landlord in the large encomiendas, had become an indispensable tool in restoring peace between the *creoles* friars and the natives.

Dodong and Yayang no longer worked in the convento. I had not seen any of the Bascons since Dodong came to see me a year ago. But I had heard talk that Yayang had given birth to a baby boy named "Jose".

Jose's looks puzzled family and friends, who described him as a Spanish mestizo, with light brown eyes. And neither Yayang nor Dodong had that much Spanish blood. I could almost hear them whispering to each other, gossiping about Jose's paternity.

Hearing this did not leave any doubt in my mind that Jose was my son.

But many times, while riding my horse around Talisay, I had to resist the strong temptation to take that turn into the Bascon farm, where I and the sisters once chased chickens for our lunch.

Deep in my heart I had built an altar for both Asay and Yayang. Before this altar I would lie prostrate and pray fervently for the two women and the children they had borne.

For Dodong I would say a special prayer of gratitude. I refrained from visiting the couple, lest I opened old wounds. They all knew they could come to me any time they needed my help. All they had to do was ask. I fervently wished that one Sunday at mass I would see the face of Asay or Yayang or Dodong lifted up to me in Holy Communion. Or, Señora Bascon's face would gaze up at me from below the pulpit.

Or, and heaven help me, I would see either of the girls in a public place with a baby in their arms.

But there was a Divine Plan, so I patiently waited for the Hand of God to strike. At the end of each busy day when I lay alone in my bed, listening to the waves and the crickets, the strong beliefs and the rigid discipline I had practiced since my youth finally brought me peace.

As though my hectic schedule were not killing enough, I was getting increasingly disturbed by the spirit of rebellion brewing around the haciendas.

One day, as I walked along a little creek in Minglanilla, I noticed a group of men gathered in a bamboo grove. Sensing danger, I stopped in my tracks and stood still behind a thick bamboo tree. I could hear the disturbing message in their discussion. I retraced my tracks, treading softly towards where I had left my horse. The last person these men wanted to encounter was me – the *administrador de haciendas*.

It was the *Tres Aliños* – three brothers in action, plotting against the Spanish rulers, especially the friars whom they wanted expelled from the colony.

The smell of rebellion was getting more acute and alarming, I realized, my heart heavy with dread. The end was near at hand. It was time to plan my moves to survive the almost certain onslaught.

A natural solution presented itself to me the following year, 1888. I was given a new assignment to the parish of Saint Francis of Assisi in Naga, the next town south of Minglanilla. Little did I expect that, here, I would meet the family who would later take me into their wing as one of them.

Now, I realize that deep in my heart this was just what I had wished for, and all my actions unconsciously led me towards that direction.

Naga was a pretty town, with a slim coastline along the beach. The blend of sky and sea in an endless expanse of blue along the main road lifted many a dampened spirit. Perfect mounds of low green hills rose just a few kilometers inland. Between these gigantic anthills, fresh water flowed freely in narrow rapids.

The parish church stood facing the sea just a few meters from the beach, and again, as in Talisay, I was lulled to sleep by the waves each night. And once more, I could take my favorite stroll along the beach to watch the sky turn ablaze in the twilight. What a welcome break from the muddy streets and little houses crowded together in the commercial district of San Nicolas.

There were only a few prominent clans in Naga and these families owned the few large haciendas there. They were both Spanish and native. From these came the political leaders of the town. This wealthy few had sent their sons and daughters to Manila or Spain to study, thus forming a class of educated natives, known as *illustrados*. The numerous tenant families of these large landholdings all added color and life to the town.

Because I worked at keeping a dignified bearing and sunny disposition, the landlords seemed to like me. I felt I blended in with them so naturally that they had taken me into their households like a family member. I spent most of my free time visiting the families in their beautiful ancestral homes.

One large prominent family, in particular, had grown fond of me and sought my continual presence in their house.

A landlord, Felix Reyes Suarez, and his wife, Catalina, had seven children and hundreds of relatives and friends around Naga and the neighboring towns. Señor Suarez was the present *cabeza de barangay*, a civic official designated by the church to head the town. Señora Suarez was descended from a past gobernadorcillo of Naga.

For centuries now, Naga's thriving fishing industry had attracted a continuous flow of settlers, especially from the neighboring island of Bohol, and the cabeza de barangay's strong leadership was indispensable to keep the town organized. He and the parish priest had to join forces to govern a diversified population and cope with rapid changes in a fast growing town.

NAGA, CEBU

ST. FRANCIS OF ASSISSI
NAGA, CEBU (1829)

THE PARISH OF NAGA

Naga is a coastal town just twenty kilometers south of Cebu City, with a scenic boulevard running close to the beach. The town is rich in natural resource. During the Spanish regime, Spanish galleons could be seen not far from the shore, waiting for its load of coal from the large coal mines in the hills of the town. The lucrative fishing industry has always attracted settlers from all over Cebu and as far as Bohol province since the pre-colonial era. Furthermore, the abundance of hardwood called "narra" (from which the town's name is derived) enabled the settlers to manufacture boats.

The patron saint of the parish is St. Francis of Assisi. The parish church was built in 1829 and is made of coral stone and hardwood.

Today Naga is a bustling city with a cement factory and a power plant.

CHAPTER 15

THE SUAREZ FAMILY

That night, my family was having one of their regular lavish dinners. The air before dinner was pregnant with anticipation as the guests waited for the parish priest to arrive.

"He is so handsome, so debonair", the ladies would whisper among themselves while the men pretended not to hear them. "And he is such an excellent speaker. Did you hear the sermon last Sunday? One moment I was crying, and the next, I was laughing. Oh, the moment felt so holy – and yet so hilarious! Just like a miracle."

"He should be a lawyer," someone said.

"Or a politician," another one said.

"What a pity he can't marry," this from one of the old *matronas*. "He'd have been good for my Teresita."

Everyone laughed at the woman's candor. Only the rich society matrons would dare say their thoughts aloud and get away with it.

"Poor Teresita! You dump on her everything you yourself want and can't get. Too bad you are not thirty years younger, Celia," another old lady teased. "Then you could have him for yourself."

"With all that perfume from Spain," another lady boldly remarked, "why, maybe she can still lure him into her arms."

In one corner, I listened quietly to all the talk about the priest. I had turned twenty, but I had not yet fallen in love. All I ever dreamed of was to become a nun, but when I expressed this wish to my parents, Mama wept and Papa must have been struck dumb. He did not say a word for days. They would simply miss me too much. So I decided to grant them their wish and stay home.

Besides, I thought, I had never considered myself attractive to men. I was fair-skinned, petite, and none of my features were extraordinary – certainly not a candidate for beauty queen. But being plain had its compensations. It brought out other virtues. I was always spoken of as generous.

Our house stood right at the beach, just off the main road a few meters from the church, exactly the way it stands now. It had always been a large sprawling two-story structure, built of hardwood and stone and a brick roof. But my favorite spot here was not the bedroom, nor the large living room with its valuable furniture and antiques, nor the veranda facing the sea, but the kitchen in one remote corner of the house. There, in that my haven, I forgot the rest of the world as I cooked my favorite dishes and tried new ones.

I must have been a good cook. Everyone in the family and all their guests seemed to love what I made. "It all tastes so mysterious," someone said of the food, "I've never tasted anything like it. What do you think she puts in there?"

This surprised me who had put nothing but the usual ingredients in the dishes. But my mother, Catalina, knew better. She was told by her own mother, my grandmother, that the most powerful ingredient in any dish was the cook's feelings – her laughter or her tears.

"Keep smiling, Aleja," Mama would tell me, "Don't ever remain sad for long. Thank God for all these blessings around us. Gratitude is the key to happiness. Then the food you cook will always taste wonderful, no matter what you put in it."

So I kept this winning smile on my face, and when I spoke, my voice seemed full of laughter. Anyway, this was the way I always felt.

This smile had become a fixture in my face, and that night I knew I would meet Padre Antolin with my best smile.

"*Buenas noches*, Padre," I would greet him in a voice brimming with joy, "here give me your hat and that umbrella. I'll hang them on the rack. Do come in and make yourself comfortable."

And this was exactly what I was doing on that particular night, in this room full of ladies anticipating his arrival. I waited by the door, greeted him, and took his hat and umbrella. For a fleeting second, he looked me over from head to toe and I knew he noticed that I was not very tall, with just the right height to match his medium build if the two of us danced together. What a strange idea, I caught myself thinking.

"So, what surprises have you concocted for us tonight, Aleja?" he asked me as the family and guests sat around the huge rectangular table, "hmmmm, it is unbelievable. It reminds me of my mother's cooking back in Castrogeriz. This [54]*lengua* is so soft, and the olives and *garbanchos* are just so right. But wait, there is something else I can't identify…"

"It is her laughter," Mama declared to everyone listening, "you are all having a taste of Aleja's happiness."

Padre Antolin nodded as though he completely understood Mama's esoteric mumbo jumbo. Everyone held their spoons in midair and waited for him to say something smart. The silence was becoming deafening.

"Aleja knew you were coming to dinner, Padre," an old matron teased the priest, "you are her hero as well as mine. And we are all having a taste of her happiness."

Everyone laughed heartily, all except me. I felt my face crumple and I must have looked like I was about to cry.

"You must be very proud of your daughter, Señor Felix," Padre Antolin came to my rescue. "And thank you, Aleja. You have made so many people happy tonight."

The ladies quickly shifted to the latest gossip, and the men started talking about the latest news. One of the distinguished guests, Diego, who had just arrived from Madrid, updated everyone on the latest political situation in Europe. He was one of those *ilustrados,* a new class of educated natives, who just acquired his *Bachiller en Artes* degree at the

University of Sto. Tomas in Manila, then gone on to Spain for cultural immersion.

Diego was the son of native tenants, but his father branched out and made a dozen fishing boats out of the [55] *narra* trees in their farm. Soon after that, the family found themselves engaged in the building of fishing boats to sell. The business had prospered to that day. *Narra* trees grew in abundance here in Naga and provided ample material for crafts and furniture.

Theirs was a typical case of the native gentry's economic advancement from agriculture to trade and commerce.

Diego stood tall and erect and confident, a young man full of promise. His piercing dark eyes shone intensely from a brown face, a perfect picture of the emerging native intelligentsia worthy of respect. He exuded authority as he told everyone about the drastic changes in the European political atmosphere since the French revolution of 1798. He explained to us the concept of democracy and freedom and how it was tearing the monarchy apart bit by bit.

"The spirit of democracy seems to win in places where there is a strong middle class. That's the reason why it won't easily take root in Spain, where the absence of a middle class leaves the monarchy unchallenged. Here in this colony, Filipinas, we have a fast growing middle class," he preached, while everyone listened enthralled at his eloquence.

"You would not believe who I met on the boat on the way here from Manila," he added to prove his point. "A young man named Salvador introduced himself to me. He said his father has been doing carpentry for all you ladies here in Naga for many years now. His name is Anselmo, and I happen to remember he and his team built our farmhouse. Salvador has just finished a *Bachiller en Artes* at Santo Tomas, just like many of us. Can you believe it – Anselmo's son – getting a college education in Manila?"

"Anselmo must have worked hard at it for years. I've seen the wonders he makes out of *narra*, especially the carved furniture. The old native folks give the education of their children prime importance.

These educated natives are forming the new middle class, and it is they who will call for reforms," one of the men replied, "Educating their children is their only hope, and the hope of this colony".

"If only we could accomplish things without bloodshed," said another gentleman. "But we have to be prepared for the worst."

"The Spanish American colonies and Mexico acquired their independence, not without bloodshed," Papa chimed in, "and in the French Revolution, monarchs were led to the guillotine to be beheaded. We all need to pray as we have been taught by the very conquerors from whom we seek our freedom."

Why do I remember all this intellectual mumbo-jumbo? The simple girl that I was at that time? *Mi amor Antolin*, as I was to call him later in life, kept repeating it to me for years. He was always trying to raise my way of thinking to a higher level. And he succeeded.

"What do you think, Padre Antolin?" someone asked the Padre.

"History will tell us that any kind of drastic change often comes with violence in varying degrees," answered Padre Antolin, "considering the natural cycle of creation-destruction-regeneration. A common example would be the remodeling of a house. One has to destroy some parts of the house before it can be rebuilt anew. One can't simply rebuild over an old obsolete structure. Consider a human life. One is born, one gets old and dies, then rises from the ashes and is reborn. The aging and the dying are difficult processes, but it is necessary for rebirth."

His little speech was followed by silence around the dinner table. Apparently, Padre Antolin could not convey such a deep message in his limited *Binisaya*. He had to revert to Spanish to express his thoughts. But Diego, fresh from his trip to Spain, soon came to his rescue and translated his words to Binisaya.

"Then, what do you suggest we do, Padre?" one of the ladies asked.

"Each one of us must open ourselves up to change. Change is necessary for growth – spiritual, physical, social," the Padre answered in Spanish. "Resisting the necessary changes often invites violence. So, let go and leave it to God. The evolution of Mankind and of the World, as manifested in World History, is a result of His Divine Will and Idea."

And Diego promptly translated his words into Binisaya, contributing his own ideas to the philosophy just said.

The sound of waves and wind coming through the large windows encouraged the Padre to go on talking.

"True freedom means being attuned to God's Will. Any other kind of freedom is false," the Padre added, very calm and composed and sure of himself.

Everyone sat still, trying to absorb the lecture. Only the sound of the wind broke through the utter silence.

"I know the truth – God's Will – can be difficult to accept. To give up one's comfortable life in order to give in to change – to accept the truth – requires utmost humility," the Padre added, in a much lower voice, like he was not so sure of his words.

"Courage…" he said further, in a barely audible whisper.

The silence around the room was palpable.

Then someone clapped his hand – it was Diego. The next moment, the Padre was surrounded by a wild applause. He smiled and gave a little bow.

"We must reexamine the role of 'masters' and 'slaves'," Diego said. "I know how difficult it must be for the masters to relinquish their roles and their possessions. But they had better start changing their posture. I am sure the Padre here can teach us a lot about the spirit of Christian detachment."

Padre Antolin turned his head and met my eyes. He must have felt me staring at him. Both our eyes locked for a few moments before I felt my cheeks grow hot and averted my gaze. Much later in our lives, he would tell me he had not forgotten that look of naked adoration in my eyes, and quietly resolved to tread softly there.

But Mama, who did not miss anything, had seen the interchange. She later told me she felt a delicious mix of fear and excitement at the sight of Padre Antolin's Achilles heel.

"Padre," Mama, clever woman, took the Padre aside as he left the house, "you must be a good cook. I know how you Spaniards are. You are all such gourmets," I heard her say, standing tall and erect in her long black lace dress, her light Spanish eyes sparkling in the gas light.

"*Si, si,*" the Padre answered - too eagerly, I thought, "I've been missing those delicious tapas and omelets my mother used to make for us."

"Tapas... and omelets!" Mama exclaimed, "why didn't I think of that? Chorizos, tuna, olives, tomatoes, onions – little bits of them in a toothpick and immersed in white wine – and those omelets – scrambled with ham and cheese and sweet pepper – ah, Padre, you must teach us how to make those."

"I could come here sometime, perhaps on Sunday afternoon, and have a long cooking session with you and the girls," the Padre proposed.

"Will you? Aleja would be in heaven. Sunday afternoon it is then."

"And we could bake some bread. I'll bring the flour and everything else we need," the Padre added.

---

[54] *ox tongue stewed in sauce with potatoes, carrots, bell pepper*
[55] *brown hardwood perfect for furniture*

CHAPTER 16

ALEJA

So I, the parish priest, turned into a gourmet cook in cooking sessions with Señora Suarez and her daughters on Sunday afternoons. The following months after that dinner in their house found me demonstrating to the women different versions of Spanish omelets. *Tapas* with varying ingredients were done and then the grand finale, a special *paella*.

I was surprised to find how much I enjoyed the sessions. But it was the sound of Aleja's hearty laughter which really captivated me. The girl laughed at just about everything —as the hot oil popped into her face, as raw onions stung her eyes, when the garlic got burnt. And she would never stop telling us her favorite jokes while cooking.

I had found a home.

Señor Suarez brought in his compadres and the women invited their friends for the dinner which we prepared. Wine flowed freely and the talk would become stimulating. I entertained the crowd with stories about my youth in Spain, years spent in the novitiate and the seminary. I told them about my long, arduous journey on the steamboat from Europe to Manila and how I almost died along the way.

The men and I would then end up in debates on philosophical, religious, and political subjects. In these sessions, I took the opportunity to teach them the philosophy behind religion and history.

"World history is the unfolding of God's Divine Plan," I explained to them, "everything that's happening to us now in this colony is meant to elevate us up to a higher consciousness. The evolution of mankind always goes in an upward spiral - up, then down - but never back to the same level as before - then up again..."

"And which part of the spiral is this colony now at this moment?" wondered a man known as Senior Panares, an older illustrado, tracing a circle in the air with his finger.

"Isn't it obvious? We are on a downward direction," remarked another gentleman, "but never to descend into the same level or lower than we were before. Three centuries ago - where were we? Just separate tribal groups steeped in ignorance and superstition."

I taught them the meaning of true freedom and detachment in the simplest of analogies.

"So Freedom is acting according to God's Divine Plan. The truth lies in His Will," I kept repeating until even the older women understood.

"Truth, though, can be painful. It takes utmost courage and humility to accept it," I tried to explain.

But Diego, the *illustrado*, enhanced my ideas by patiently translating my Spanish to *Binisaya* and simplifying them with stories.

"They all worship you, men and women alike," Señora Suarez indulged me with her observations. "Everyone loves your candor. You burn up with such intensity. The way your eyes flash when you get excited...it fascinates everyone, the women especially!"

One quiet evening on a weekday the entire family went to a social gathering, leaving all but Aleja home. The girl was down with a slight fever and sore throat. I decided to stay beside her to keep her company, and we both sat on the veranda fronting the sea. A gauze of clouds wrapped the huge full moon, the stars were but a hint, and the cool sea breeze blew gently in to make it a perfect night for confidences.

Aleja and I exchanged stories about our lives. I told her about my mother's death when I was a boy, how this early loss determined the direction my life took, guided more by my feelings and my intuition.

This last thought surprised me. I had always believed that I was in complete control of my life. But looking back these past years, I realized that I had done things on sheer impulse. I seem to have been driven by violent forces underneath my conscious mind. But this was the first time I had ever connected all that to my early loss in life.

So much of the human mind still remained in the dark.

"There were a few times in my life when I took drastic action without thinking, as though led by a powerful impulse beyond my control," I told her. "It is all very mysterious, the way the human mind works. Someday, perhaps in a few decades, a separate science will devote itself to the study of the human mind."

What was it about Aleja that unearthed my innermost self? She exuded such purity and peace of soul. I felt her power to feel the Unseen.

She could not match the stunning good looks of those Spanish mestizas. But she was brimming over with feminine allure. Petite but plump in the right places, she would always have the appeal of a burgeoning adolescent girl. She had oriental features – a cute little nose, almond eyes, and the fair skin of a sometime Chinese ancestor. But her most striking feature was the color of her eyes – they were light brown and fringed with long curly lashes, which betrayed a trace of Spanish ancestry. There was so much life in those little brown pools. One could drown in those eyes and lose himself in them.

"In ten years, I will be forty years old, Aleja. But even now I already feel like an old man. Just so much has happened in my short life that I feel I've already lived for a very long time," I confided to her, laughing at myself.

"You're so fortunate, Padre, to have had such a colorful life. While I have just been right here, in this little town, my greatest happiness in preparing food for other people to enjoy," she replied. "But, Padre, your life is by no means over. I have a strong feeling you are going to live for a much longer time. The world will still benefit from your wisdom and your powerful mind."

"And you, Hija, are a sweet and generous soul. You will make a wonderful wife and mother," I told her with conviction.

"Padre, Diego has proposed to me," she suddenly announced.

"Ah…did he?" was all I could utter. I was surprisingly tongue-tied. I felt a tightness in my chest. What was wrong with me?

"Ah…I am happy to hear that, Aleja. So, when is the big day?" I managed to blurt out.

Aleja could not say a word. She surely felt that I was upset. But why should I have been? It didn't make sense.

"Oh, I'm not sure, Padre," she hesitated.

"Are you not in love with him?" I asked. "Diego is a fine, young man with a bright future. He will make you a perfect husband, and you will have so many wonderful, gifted children. I would be so happy for you, Aleja."

But I did not sound happy. I think I was jealous.

"I have never fallen in love, Padre," Aleja told me. "How does that feel – that kind of love? Have you ever been in love, Padre?"

That I did not flinch at such a personal question showed how much I felt at ease with this woman.

"Yes," I replied. "I have been in love, Aleja. But in my position and with the vows I have made, that kind of love for a woman has no place."

"So how did you let her go?" she asked.

I had never asked myself this question. A few seconds passed before I could give her a reply.

"She made it easier for me. She just left. I did not know where she had gone. I have not heard from her since," I finally told her.

"What a brave woman!" Aleja exclaimed. "Her love for you was so unselfish, and I think that's what they call 'true love'."

"Yes, just like the unconditional love of a mother," I told her.

"I am not going to marry Diego, Padre," Aleja announced. "My parents are going to be displeased, especially Mama who can't wait to have more grandchildren."

I could merely nod. I was suddenly very tired and sleepy.

"I must go home now, Hija. It's getting late, and I have early morning mass tomorrow," I took my leave.

CHAPTER 17

DARKNESS AND LIGHT

And so Naga continued to prosper before my eyes – the boat industry, the fishing and the farming, and most especially the coal mines in the barrio of Alpaco. There had been a huge demand for coal in the past decades with the advent of the steam engine which had powered the steamboats and the trains, and cargoboats from other parts of the colony came to the Naga seaport to pick up coal.

As parish priest, I went to Alpaco regularly to visit the miners' village and say mass there. Until this day, Alpaco is a remote barrio deep in the mountains of Naga. I and my assistant would take our horses and ride along the riverbanks through banana groves and sugar cane fields. The river in this area was so large it was almost a lake. But in the warm summers, it was dry, except for a trickle of water running in the middle of a wide sandy surface. The sky over this vast flat land stretched infinitely all the way to the distant hills. In its midst, one strongly felt the eternal, the endless, the undying.

Ten miles into this flat land, we would guide our horses up the low hills into the mines. The trip took us a full two hours. But we made stops along the way to rest and feast on wild guavas growing abundantly along the hillsides. I looked forward to these wild guavas like a little child anticipating his favorite cookie. Surrounded by nature's bounty, I felt the usual joy which renewed my depleted energies.

Energy was certainly what I needed to face the sad conditions surrounding the miners. Many of these laborers were convicts, prisoners on forced labor, paid with very low wages, poorly fed, under the worst of working conditions. They worked under the ground, inhaling coal dust, with hardly any fresh air coming in.

I could only console them with words during my sermon, delivered amidst a chorus of hard coughing among the congregation. All to no avail, as the men looked up at me with eyes devoid of expression. I had never seen a sea of sad faces nor felt so much human misery concentrated in one small area like this tiny chapel.

One mid morning, as I delivered my sermon, I felt the air grow heavy. I looked around the congregation while I talked but did not see anything strange. The feeling became more intense. I started to feel nauseous. Whatever it was seemed to be choking me.

Then I saw it. A man stood out from the crowd in the front pew. One minute he wasn't there, and the next, there he was. He was slim, small, with a youthful face, but strangely, his beard was waist long and white like that of a very old man. His eyes were a pair of fiery slits as his gaze burned into me. The sermon over, I turned around to face the altar and say the Latin prayers out loud. The hair in my neck and arms stood on end as I felt the same disturbing stare, and my voice broke and faltered. When I again faced the crowd to distribute Holy Communion, I felt relieved of the weight and found that the strange man was nowhere to be seen.

After the mass, as I turned to bless the congregation, I glimpsed the same man standing in another side of the chapel, with the same burning stare directed at me. My hands shook as I blessed the crowd with the sign of the cross.

"Go after that little man," I told my assistant immediately after mass, as the strange figure walked out of the chapel.

"He went into the cave under the *Dakit* tree," my assistant reported later. "Padre, you must know that *Dakit* trees are enchanted. They are inhabited by powerful spirits."

I was convinced that I had seen a demon. This was not surprising to find one in a place where there was so much human suffering. The Dark Forces were always ready to engulf those who were weakened by despair.

In spite of my fears, I resolved to fight this darkness pervading the mines. But the only weapon I had was the Word. The Word of God was the best I could offer to restore the workers' faith. I decided to spend more time in this dreadful place.

But my noble intentions were soon aborted as I came home to find a letter informing me of my official transfer to the parish of Minglanilla.

CHAPTER 18

THE RESOLUTE WOMAN

After the Padre left, I stayed alone in the veranda an hour longer, reflecting on all that had been said. Was I imagining it, or did the Padre have this little jealous note in his voice when I broke the news about Diego?

That jealous note led me to come to a big decision – I was not going to marry Diego or anyone else.

And at that exact moment, I felt a quickening in my gut. An early feotus in the womb must move like that, I imagined. That evening, I felt like my life would never be the same again.

Then, one day, Padre Antolin broke the news to the little party gathered in our house.

"In a few months I will have a new assignment – at the Minglanilla Parish," he announced. I felt my face sag as I heard the news.

"Nothing is going to change. I will certainly come and visit your family as often as possible. That's for certain. You all have made me feel one with you. How could I stay away from you ever?" he reassured us. "Besides, how can I live without your cooking?"

"Let's have a despedida for the Padre," Mama suggested, trying to sound happy in a voice heavy with sadness. "Let's hold a dinner and dance at the rotunda in Carcar. Everyone enjoys that nice band there.

And it would be so convenient for the Duterte's, the Pañares's, and our many Carcar relatives."

"Oh, that would be so lovely. I love that band," one of the old aunts clasped her wrinkled hands, "Padre, will you dance with me? Please? Then I can die in peace."

Everyone finally laughed merrily, including me, who did not miss a waltz number.

"Now, I can wear my new lace *terno*," said another aging matron.

I tried not to laugh at the thought of this short, bent old woman in an exquisite long *mestiza* gown with the huge butterfly sleeves. But such was the spirit of these rich matrons.

"And Aleja, you must wear the pink embroidered silk gown. Remember, the one which Diego brought you from Spain? And that pretty pearl necklace," one of my sisters said. "And please, we must not forget to invite Diego."

"Ah, would that not be a good time to announce Aleja's and Diego's engagement?" asked Mama, "what do you think, Aleja?"

"Mama, I have decided not to marry Diego," I declared, careful to keep my voice flat and my face impassive. I steeled myself for the onslaught certain to follow my pronouncement.

Everyone, including Padre Antolin, was too stunned to speak.

"I am never going to get married," I continued. Suddenly, I was filled with bravado. "I am going to be happy exactly where I am now."

Mama stared at me for a few seconds, her face distorted with shock and disbelief. She opened her mouth to say something, but failed to find the words. She finally ran out of the room, followed by one of my sisters. The rest of the women sat dumbstruck for an eternal minute, then prepared to leave as well, leaving only me and the Padre rooted to the same spot.

The Padre and I looked at each other for a second. Then we burst into a quiet, controlled laughter.

"You will have to dance with me at the despedida, Padre Antolin. Start practicing the waltz," I told him.

"Hija, everyone will be shocked," he answered, still laughing.

"Padre, if you can dance with ancient Lola Corazon and other ancients like her, nobody will even care if I sneak in a few steps," I told him, with a wave of my hand.

"Alright then, I will try to borrow the proper attire from one of the men. Perhaps Diego has one of those *barong tagalogs?*" he answered, "He is just my size."

"So, why don't we practice right now?" I startled him with the suggestion. "Da dan, step, step, da dan, step, step, da dan, step, step..." I sang, as I waltzed around the room.

The Padre took off his habit and stood there in his cotton shirt and black pants. With a sweep of his hand, he executed a dramatic bow, took me by the hand, and led me to the open space in the living room.

"Ay, [56]*Dios mio!*" Mama exclaimed, almost fainting with shock as she came into the room and found me and the Padre dancing.

"Come on, Ma, why don't you join us?" I asked her, laughing gaily.

---

[56] *My god! In Spanish*

CHAPTER 19

MINGLANILLA, THE BREWING CAULDRON

The year 1891 found me in my new assignment at the Minglanilla Parish, happy that I was back on grounds familiar to me as the past administrator of the friar estates there. Having found a home with the Suarez's in the neighboring town of Naga, I felt confident that I would never be alone again for the rest of my life. No matter what happened to me in these uncertain times, this home would always be there to welcome me.

Formerly just a "visita" of the Talisay Parish, the former baranggay Buat was renamed Minglanilla in 1857. On the same year, a new parish church was built on top of a hill a hundred meters from the main highway, marking it as an independent parish. The population around the towns had increased considerably in the past decades, with people from the neighboring islands of Negros, Bohol, Leyte, and Mindanao settling in Cebu. Just on any Sunday, I and my assistants had to perform as much as four baptisms, one or two weddings, added to several masses.

There was, however, a more urgent need for my presence at Minglanilla. The church haciendas suffered from yet another big challenge - a big drought which dried up the rice lands and caused massive crop failure. The following year, a strong typhoon hit and uprooted many of banana trees, with fruits hanging from them. The strong winds also destroyed farm houses and left entire families living in makeshift structures. A lot of goats, sensitive to water, perished, and the homeless chickens roamed in all directions.

The cruel climate only aggravated the insidious spirit of rebellion, the atmosphere around the haciendas heavily charged with discontent and anger among the tenants.

I had been told the names of the perpetrators and I knew some of them from my long exposure as the administrator of these haciendas. They were good, hardworking men and I was ready to listen to their grievances. Now famous for advocacy, I was again the one entrusted with the task of trouble shooting.

The spirit of change was getting increasingly more palpable with each day. I could feel it most when I went to public places like the market. The common folk greeted me with their eyes averted, their voices betraying an unmistakable undercurrent. Gone were the adoring looks, the tone of respect and reverence, and in its place was naked ridicule and contempt the moment I turned my back.

I felt utterly sad at this turn of events. When all was said and done, the friars had contributed so much good to this society. They had always been scarce in numbers, yet the few stretched their capabilities to the limit in enriching the culture - through religion, the arts, education, the environment, governance. Most of all, we friars had been responsible for the character formation of the people, both as individuals and as groups.

I could not deny that some of us friars had strayed from the path of righteousness. Even I himself was far from exempt. Yet, it was simply unjust to judge the entire group with the conduct of a minority. Even some native priests, human as they were, were found guilty of abusive practices, given the same situation as the friars. Yet such cases were all but ignored by the natives.

At this point, we had been briefed of some alarming developments in Manila. A secret society was being formed by Dr. Jose Rizal, an *illustrado* who went around Europe for further studies after obtaining a medical degree from the University of Sto. Tomas. He and other Filipinos in Madrid and around Europe had been exposed to the same philosophies of freedom which incited the French Revolution and the ones in the Americas. They were a group of native intelligentsia aiming towards social reforms through peaceful means. They were the ones who spread propaganda, accusing us friars for using our power and our resources to thwart the activities of the *illustrados* like them. Thus they have asked for the expulsion of the friars and the installation of native priests in their place

Inmaculate Heart of Mary Parish in Minglanilla,
Cebu built in 1878

THE PARISH OF MINGLANILLA: *The present building has
replaced the one built in 1878.*

*The town of Minglanilla, some 20 kms from the City of Cebu, was
just a barrio of Talisay in the Spanish colonial era until it became a
separate parish in 1857 when the church was built. The entire Talisay-
Minglanilla area was a huge 8000-hectare Talisay-Minglanilla friar
estates belonging to the Friar Orders until the massive land-reform of
the early 1900's under the new American regime.*

*Towards the end of the nineteenth century, the hills of Minglanilla
housed rebels preparing for the insurrection against the Spanish
Regime.*

*Today Minglanilla is a progressive city with its hills filled with housing
projects.*

These *illustrados* had been educated in schools and universities founded by the friar orders, I thought with some bitterness. And at this point, they had turned against their own mentors. I recalled how much time and energy I myself had devoted to this society, expecting little in return for my own self. And I had felt absolute fulfillment in these sacred tasks.

I loved this colony and the people in it, and I, as a minister, felt a deep pride every time I encountered a talented and accomplished native – like Diego, for one. Yet these illustrados felt that we, who had formed their minds and their spirits, had also betrayed them. My home country, Spain, and the Spaniards who came to this colony had the noblest of intentions. In the end, all of them would be judged according to the few who abused their power.

With my extensive education and exposure, I always remained open to change. But change always comes at a great price. Nevertheless, the burden of my sadness made me anxious and weary and my daily taks harder to bear.

But an occasional silver lining always appeared through the stormy clouds. An ancestral land, which was grabbed by a Spanish encomendero in the past century, was suddenly returned to the descendants of the rightful owners.

Manoy Sidro, the tenant of the Haciendas de Talisay I have mentioned earlier, just could not believe his good fortune.

Señor Pedro, the neighboring encomendero, infamous for his abuses to the natives, had long been stricken with complications from a brainstroke. The first stroke left him paralyzed in one side of his body. Another stroke a few months later left him mindless, drooling, and incontinent, unable to swallow his food. Exactly on cue, all the household help left without a word, confirming the long drawn-out insidious campaign against the Spaniards.

Perhaps because of his impotence or because, without a proper bath, he smelled like a goat, Señor Pedro's mistress of many years ran off with a young farm hand. She had taken away her little daughter by Señor Pedro, whom the old man adored. With this final blow, Señor

Pedro had a third stroke which left him totally blind. Doña Carmen, his wife, had to attend to him herself morning, noon, and night. The old woman was spared any more agony when her husband had a fatal heart attack.

Doña Carmen then proceeded to settle their estates after her husband died. With all their grown children living in Spain, this old Spanish lady was just longing to spend the rest of her life in the bosom of her mother land.

"I've decided to return the land which our ancestors grabbed from yours, Sidro," she announced to a startled Sidro, as I sat with the two of them in her large veranda. "I am fully aware of the legend between your family and mine, of how my husband's ancestors grabbed much of your ancestors' land. I have heard stories about the abused women, as well. This is how some of your relatives are descended from Pedro's ancestors".

I sat there, the role of mediator and translator weighing down on me, as I tried to get the profound message across as clearly as possible.

"The pain and anguish which we have inflicted on you and your family for generations is too great," she added. "The long terrible illness that my husband, Pedro, suffered was obviously caused by the forces of karma. The burden of that injustice should not befall my children. God help us! So I have taken it into my hands to return the lands to you."

I hesitated at the words "karma", at how to explain "karma" in Binisaya.

[57] "*Gabá*," Sidro told me much later, supplying the word as he understood it from context. [58]"*Nahadlok si Senora ug gaba para sa iyang familia*."

Amazing how spoken words could be deciphered just from the tone! *Gaba* meant "retribution" for a bad deed but did not include reward for the good.

Sidro went down on his knees before the Spanish lady and thanked her, tears falling down his cheeks. At long last, his ancestors had been avenged.

"*Salamat*, Padre," Sidro thanked me after Doña Carmen left. "What has happened is clearly a miracle." I told Sidro how the Holy Spirit worked wonders.

Actually – and this is something I could never tell Sidro or anyone - Doña Carmen had been coming to me in confession, whispering softly through the screen separating us.

"I'm afraid of the hand of God," she had told me. "I have had a choking fear of just about everything around me, Padre. I am terrified of the mosquitoes. Every time one bites me, and this happens a lot, I feel certain I am going to die. And butterflies! Padre, even the butterflies frighten me. There are the brown ones who might be the spirits of the dead come to avenge us."

"Only God's grace erases all fear. God is merciful, but He is also just," I told her and gave her some advice – how she could put matters right - which she had then followed to the letter.

The news of Sidro's story soon spread throughout Minglanilla and the neighboring towns. Though I was happy for Sidro, I was sad to note how Doña Carmen's good deed had ignited the flame of rebellion even more around the haciendas. Recalled anew were the numerous cases of landgrabbing by the *encomenderos*, and even by the friars, gone unchecked through the centuries. Anger and bitterness, long buried, had now been unearthed.

Thus was I besieged by such angry natives who came to consult me, airing out their grievances with tiresome histrionics. They had come, not only from Minglanilla and Talisay, but also from the other towns, as far away as Argao in the south. It seemed that my readiness for advocacy had become a legend far and wide.

I soon found myself going to the distant towns in my horse and carriage to intercede for the natives, faced with *encomenderos* who stubbornly refused to listen.

"These natives have never been in a position to take care of their lands the way we have cared for them. We have created miracles out of the wilderness they claim their ancestors own," was a favorite line among the encomenderos. "We can't just give up so easily. We have all it takes, all the men and all the weapons, to use force if we have to."

If only all encomenderos were like Doña Carmen, who was wise enough to learn her lessons from life's turn of events! If only men of any color and creed were less attached to greed and power! Then, change would come without bloodshed.

---

[57] Wrath, as in Wrath of God, in Binisaya
[58] The madame is afraid that divine wrath would befall her family, in Binisaya

CHAPTER 20

※

FIDELINA

August was fast approaching and soon I found no time or energy to dwell on advocacy as I managed the frantic preparations for the Minglanilla town fiesta celebrations.

August 22, 1892. That afternoon I found myself in the midst of the fiesta celebration in the Church Square, attended by the Bishop, the neighboring parish priests, and the civic officials of Minglanilla, Naga, Talisay, and the ciudad.

I will never forget that magical hour for the rest of my life.

After the dance presentation, during a short break before the large banquet, I stood beneath a large tree to talk to the guests. Towards dusk, the sky was blazing with tongues of fire. Twilight time had always been a witching hour for me, and the last guest left me there standing by myself, feeling that same nostalgia creeping in my heart.

"I am so exhausted," I realized, sighing quietly, gulping more of the breeze which blew in from the fields around.

Suddenly, I felt something tugging at my habit. Startled, I looked down to see a little girl's face looking up at me. I started to say something but words escaped me. Can it be? It was my sister Olimpia!

Then, I realized that Olimpia had grown up. And this little girl seemed not more than six years old. But she had the same long, black hair cascading down her back. Her hair was wild, curly, exactly as Olimpia's hair had looked.

"Hello!" I greeted her in Binisaya, "how are you?"

The little girl's face crumpled. She began to cry. I realized she was lost.

"Where is your mother?" I asked her gently. But she violently shook her head and cried louder, her breasts heaving with violent sobs. Then she ran away.

I walked after her as fast as I could. Passersby stared at us, startled at the sight of the priest in his white habit chasing after the little girl in a white dress. But I was again fifteen years old, running around, chasing butterflies with a five-year-old Olimpia. It all seemed surreal. I thought I had gone through a time warp.

"*Hija! Hija!* Please don't run," I kept calling out to her.

"Peding! Peding!" a woman's voice called out from the direction of the church steps.

The little girl ran faster towards the voice.

"Mama! Mama!" she called out.

The woman's face was blocked by the baby she was carrying. At the sound of the little girl's voice, she turned around.

It was her! I froze in my tracks for a few moments. Then I walked towards the woman and the two children, my heart beating hard against my chest. Though I could hardly breathe, I knew I looked calm and composed.

"Asay!"

I could only whisper her name as I extended my hand. A few seconds passed before she took my hand and shook it weakly. Her face was crumpled as she tried to hold back her tears.

"Asay," I said again, my voice weak with emotion, "everything's alright now. Your little girl has been found."

Then tears copiously gushed down her cheeks, and she wiped them off with the little baby's dress. I offered her my handkerchief. She took it without hesitation.

"Cry it all out, Hija," I told her gently, "it will make you feel better."

Saying these words, I felt like an old fool. I stood rooted to one spot quietly, waiting for the crying to subside. The world around me seemed unreal. I felt unreal.

"I'm sorry, Padre," she finally found her voice, "Fidelina is just a bit too adventurous. I should have left her at home with my mother."

"No, don't be sorry. You don't realize how happy I am to see you, Asay – you and your little ones," I heard myself saying. "So, how are you?"

"We're fine," she answered in a breathless whisper, as though she had lost her voice. "somebody invited us over for the fiesta."

"I see," I answered, "I am so glad that you came. And I hope you are staying for the banquet."

My words sounded like a regular textbook-perfect language lesson.

"Nicolasa!" a male voice called out from behind me, "Ah, Padre Frias. *Buenas Noches.* I see you and Nicolasa have met. We are all here for the fiesta celebration. I have come to represent our schoolmaster at the Cathedral. You must know Señor Pepe Montecillo. He is down with a fever."

The man spoke to me in Spanish. I recognized him as a certain Juan, whose last name I could not recall. He was a creole from Argentina - not a fully ordained priest, but a lay Brother who had enough training to assist in the parishes and teach in parochial schools.

"I am Juan Asuiaca. This beautiful little girl is Fidelina, Nicolasa's daughter. And this adorable baby is her second daughter, Corazon," Juan introduced the two children. "Corazon is my child."

And Fidelina? Who is her father? I promptly swallowed my words.

"Come, Fidelina," I offered my hand to Fidelina. "May I just spend a few minutes with your little girl?" I asked Asay. She nodded, and I led the little girl into the church, leaving Asay and Juan at the door.

"Come, Hija, let me show you where I work," I said, as I showed Fidelina around the large church. She followed me meekly, like a little lamb. I prayed a barely audible Hail Mary as we stood in front of the statue of the Virgin Mary. Then we sat in front of the main altar for a full five minutes.

As the bright lights from the altar shone on Fidelina's eyes, I saw how much like my mother's they were - brown and green battling for supremacy.

"She's going to be a beauty. And a strong, assertive one - a fighter just like my mother, Luisa," I told myself, feeling an indescribable father's joy.

Finally, it was time to say goodbye. I brought her back to her mother and Juan. I just knew I would see her again.

"*Muchas gracias,*" I told Asay. More words would have ruined the simple message.

"*Muchas gracias,*" she smiled brightly. She returned my handkerchief, soaked with her tears. "I want you to have this," she said as she turned around and left, holding Fidelina with one hand while Juan carried the baby Corazon.

They looked like an odd couple, with him a good four inches shorter than she. Only then did I notice how pretty she looked in a long skirt printed with large red flowers and a sheer white lace *kimona*. What a long way from a man's white shirt and trousers she used to wear! I swallowed hard at the memory.

"She has grown more appealing with age, with the same beauty shining from within," I thought, as I crumpled the tear-soaked handkerchief.

I went back to the altar and fell on my knees in one dark corner of the church. There was nothing in my mind and in my heart but an overwhelming mixture of strong emotions – a strange cocktail of sadness and happiness, a touch of gratitude, a sense of my own mortality, and finally a glimpse of immortality.

"All this will come to pass. Someday I will surely leave this world. But something of me will remain 'til the end of time." I finally told myself.

"Thank you, my lord God."

Then I put on the garment of the shepherd and went out into the evening to celebrate with my flock.

DISCUSSION V
The Search Continues

March, 2014
Cebu City

Fidelin, Becky, and I sit across one another, feasting on barbecue, rice, and broiled fish while discussing our latest find.

*"Amazing how **the** Mormons have made it their mission to trace everyone's family tree all over the world," I said. "So, this afternoon, we really found some exciting data on Antolin Frias and Lola Asay."*

We had just spent an afternoon at the Mormon Temple in Cebu searching their records under **Family Tree.com** *for any data on the Frias and Bascon familes.*

"Padre Antolin's parents were **Juan Frias and Luisa Ramos.** *But we already know that from Joy's trip to Valladolid," Becky remarked.*

"Yes, but their names helped us identify **Olimpia Frias,** *Antolin's sister. We have just found records of her marriage to* **Fernando Alonso,** *in which the parents of the bride - her parents - are listed as Juan Frias and Luisa Ramos, same as Antolin's. So, tonight, we uncovered that Antolin had a sister. Isn't that great?" I said. "However, his siblings are not listed in his school records at Valladolid. One will have to dig up the registry in*

his hometown, Castrogeriz," I added. "Castrogeriz is just two hours by bus away from Valladolid. Anyone interested in going?"

"But, at least, we have found Olimpia and in addition to that, the marriage records of her son, **Juan Frias Alonso**— named after her father— coming from Rio de Janeiro," Fidelin contributed, "Now we know we have a branch of the family in Brazil".

"Singing the Bossa Nova," I joked. "What fun!"

"Equally amazing was uncovering **Corazon Bascon's** marriage records. She married **Guillermo Chan** at the Manila Metropolitan Cathedral, and her parent's are listed as **Juan Asuiaca and Nicolasa Bascon.** We have all known Lola Corazon, Lola Peding's half-sister, the second child of Lola Asay. But who knew who her father was? Now we know it was Jaime," I said.

"I looked up the name Asuiaca in Google and found it concentrated around Argentina," I continued. "I remember Papa Bastian telling me that, after Frias, Lola Asay had a child by another minister, although not an ordained priest. I guess we can presume that Juan was one of those creoles from Mexico and South America who came to the Philippines to be priests' assistants."

"It's really interesting how you can just put all the missing pieces together with a few important clues," said Becky. "And so what about Lola Corazon? What happened to her after she got married?"

"The **Chan** couple had several children and lived a comfortable life in the vicinity of Sampaloc, an old business district in Manila," I told her. "Lola Peding and her sister were close. They were Nicolasa Bascon's only children."

"Lola Asay had wonderful children. They were strong women and thrived well in spite of the challenging times," Becky said.

"That's how it all seems," we all nodded out heads in agreement.

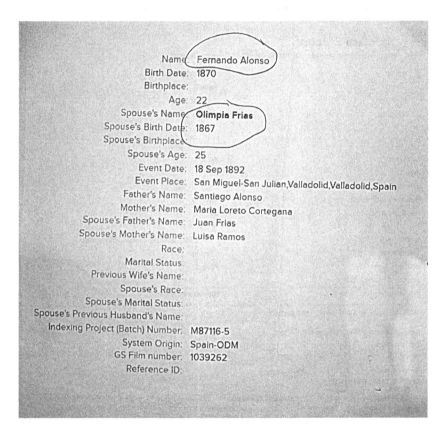

Name: Fernando Alonso
Birth Date: 1870
Birthplace:
Age: 22
Spouse's Name: Olimpia Frias
Spouse's Birth Date: 1867
Spouse's Birthplace:
Spouse's Age: 25
Event Date: 18 Sep 1892
Event Place: San Miguel-San Julian,Valladolid,Valladolid,Spain
Father's Name: Santiago Alonso
Mother's Name: Maria Loreto Cortegana
Spouse's Father's Name: Juan Frias
Spouse's Mother's Name: Luisa Ramos
Race:
Marital Status:
Previous Wife's Name:
Spouse's Race:
Spouse's Marital Status:
Spouse's Previous Husband's Name:
Indexing Project (Batch) Number: M87116-5
System Origin: Spain-ODM
GS Film number: 1039262
Reference ID:

MARRIAGE RECORDS OF OLIMPIA FRIAS, SISTER OF
ANTOLIN FRIAS

familytree.com

Nicolasa Bascon

mentioned in the record of Guillermo Chan and Covaron Bascon

Name	Nicolasa Bascon
Gender	Female
Husband	Juan Asuiaca
Daughter	Covaron Bascon

Name	Guillermo Chan
Birth Date	1879
Age	35
Spouse's Name	Covaron Bascon
Spouse's Birth Date	1889
Spouse's Age	25
Event Date	16 Jan 1914
Event Place	Manila, Metropolitan Manila, Philippines
Father's Name	Chan Fos Kay
Mother's Name	Pang She
Spouse's Father's Name	Juan Asuiaca
Spouse's Mother's Name	**Nicolasa Bascon**

PHILIPPINES MARRIAGES, 1723-1957

Indexing Project (Batch) Number	I05779-5
System Origin	Philippines-EASy
GS Film number	1495715
Reference ID	34063

CITING THIS RECORD

"Philippines Marriages, 1723-1957," database, *FamilySearch* (https://familysearch.org/ark:/61903/1:1:FNQK-SZB : accessed 13 May 2016), Nicolasa Bascon in entry for Guillermo Chan and Covaron Bascon, 16 Jan 1914; citing Manila, Metropolitan Manila, Philippines, reference 34063; FHL microfilm 1,495,715.

MARRIAGE RECORDS OF CORAZON BASCON, DAUGHTER OF NICOLASA BASCON AND JUAN ASUIACA

familytree.com

CHAPTER 21

UNLEASHED FURY

The situation around the haciendas worsened as the tenants became increasingly rebellious and refused to pay their dues to the friar owners. Losing the revenue from the lands, the friars had no choice but to collect dues for masses, funerals, weddings, novenas, baptisms, and other services – which were granted for free before this time.

This new practice diminished their public persona even more and reinforced the popular belief that they continued to enrich themselves at the expense of the poor natives. The clamor for the replacement by native priests grew louder.

1892. I had heard alarming news which confirmed my fears of open rebellion and bloodshed. A society called the KKK - *Katipunan, Kalayaan, Kagalang-galangan Ng Mga Anak Ng Bayan* - had just been founded in Manila, with Andres Bonifacio as its leader.

By 1896, Spanish Governor Gen. Blanco was recalled and replaced by Governor Polavieja, whose inhuman tyranny only managed to ignite the flames still further.

1896 August. The revolution finally started in Manila. This was followed by a Reign of Terror of mass executions and exiles of the suspected leaders and participants. Polavieja ordered the execution of Dr. Jose Rizal in Manila on Dec. 30, 1896.

The following year, 1897, Andres Bonifacio himself was executed and Emilio Aguinaldo had replaced him as the revolutionary leader. But, soon, a peace treaty, the Pact of Biak-na-Bato, was signed between the Katipuneros and the Spanish government, and Aguinaldo and his leaders were exiled in Hongkong.

Meanwhile, Glicerio Canonigo, the first Gobernadorcillo of Naga in Cebu, and Marcelo de la Cerna, Captain of the Guards, had turned rebel against the Spaniards

In the towns of Talisay and Minglanilla, in the midst of the large Talisay-Minglanilla Friar Lands, the tenants talked of nothing else but their up and coming liberation from the oppressors. I had heard from reliable sources that the tenants had been manufacturing weapons – bolos, knives, sling shots – this last one was pathetic - for the coming uprising in Cebu. There were rumors of a revolutionary army being secretly formed among the native workmen in the town of San Nicolas.

Gentle and sensitive by nature, I had always abhorred the use of force. I grew up in a land surrounded by meek sheep and wheat bowing to the wind, its master, with a mind attuned to the rest of creation. The prospect of violence proved too overwhelming for me and it took enormous willpower to keep myself from breaking apart at the seams.

As the situation around the Friar haciendas took a turn for the worse, I was finally relieved of my duties as parish priest of Minglanilla in 1891. Now, I was ordered to devote whatever little was left of my energies for the gargantuan task of monitoring the haciendas for signs of rebellion.

One evening, exhausted from a grueling day at the rice lands, where I had to settle a violent boundary dispute between tenants, I found an envelope at the doorstep to the convento. My hands shook as I opened it.

"Padre," the letter said in Binisaya, "you and others in your position must leave this town and this colony. You have caused immeasurable suffering upon us whom you call 'indios'. You have stolen our lands, abused our women, unjustly exploited our resources..." the letter went on enumerating cases of so-called abuse, with names of the "abused" women.

"…and you, Padre Antolin, how could you do that to those women? You are no more than a beast! They are not just any two women. They are sisters! For this you must burn in hell, as you friars have always taught us, *indios*. You must be grateful that we are giving you ample warning to just leave and save your life," and with this the letter ended unsigned.

My knees buckling, I fell on the front steps and sat there with the letter in my hands. I then felt someone out there watching me in the surrounding darkness.

The letter sounded like it had been written by someone educated. That new batch of educated natives - those *illustrados* – were the true challenge! Their accusations hurt. Me – a beast?

In sympathy, the crickets became quiet. As the wind began to blow, the dead leaves swirled and danced around me, whispering sadly.

Memories of the past years of my life flashed before me - starting with my mother's death, my strict confinement at the seminary as a young adolescent, the long journey to the Islas, the almost inhuman burden of my work here, my personal devotion to my mission, the deprivation of my all too human needs, the lives which had flourished from my touch - and all that to be summed up into one or two all too human missteps…

Many of the women mentioned in the letter were not of minor age. They were fully grown mature women in their twenties or thirties, responsible adults all. Most of them lived comfortable lives on their own resources. They were certainly not impoverished young girls whom the friars "abused".

And why not consider that these so-called abusive relationships were actually deep friendships with lots of love and respect?

And what of the so-called "abused *indios*"? I knew too much of life in the haciendas to have seen the abuse work in both directions. Friars, lay Spanish hacienderos, and the *Indio* tenants abused each other, and this "contest" contributed to financial loss in this colony. At this point, Las Islas Filipinas was losing as a business concern for the Spanish crown.

And now for all that I had sacrificed for this society, to be summed up as a mere pervert!

But I had never been in any position to choose my duties, so after the incident I stayed rooted in my assigned tasks at Minglanilla with a heart heavy with dread.

And just as I was about to throw up my hands and give up the ghost, I got a much needed break. In 1897, I got a new assignment to the Parish of Argao, 68 kilometers from the ciudad de Cebu. I thanked God for His loving mercy.

CHAPTER 22

ARGAO, THE LAST STOP

1897. Argao is one of the oldest towns in the island, founded in the year 1608. The magnificent church still stands today as it has for the past three centuries – the same baroque-rococo architecture, paintings in the ceiling, a huge organ rumored to have been shipped direct from Mexico, an elaborate pulpit, angels all over the walls, and an exquisite statue of the patron saint – St. Michael de Archangel.

But what I loved best was the convento. After parish duties, I loved to sit around in the large parlor, luxuriating in comfortable antique furniture. The high ceilings and wide windows admitted so much sunlight and air, the sound of waves from the nearby beach, and the voices from the plaza below.

The Church and convento stood in a wide plaza surrounded by the town hall and government buildings with equally magnificent stone walls. The entire town glowed with the warm shade of red in the brick roofs.

Aside from manufacturing bricks, the town also prided itself as the weaver of some very exotic fabrics called *hablon* and *sinamay*, made of colorful dyed fiber. There were more dressmakers, silversmiths, blacksmiths, painters, carpenters, and musicians here than anywhere else I had been assigned. The artist in me was awakened in this culture of artists and artisans. The fulfilled basic human need for creative expression lent a wholesome air around the town.

But to this day as I write this, what Argao is really famous for are the "*tubâ* for Gods" and the delicious native cake called [59] *torta*.

What a welcome respite from the tension in Minglanilla! I would sigh with vast relief, as I feasted on *torta* and *tsokolate*, my regular merienda. I rejoiced in this special *tuba*, fit indeed for gods.

I felt I deserved this break as I turned forty years of age. That quiet time in my life was truly heaven sent.

ST. MICHAEL DE ARCHANGEL PARISH CHURCH
AND CONVENTO IN ARGAO, CEBU

BUILT IN 1733

Evelyn Regner Seno

THE PARISH OF ARGAO

The town of Argao, 68 kms from Cebu City, was founded in 1608. Remnants of the Spanish era are found intact in the town square. The original municipio, the Church, the convent, and the plaza transport one in time to the 1600's.

The church was built in 1733, with its patron saint St. Michael de Archangel. The baroque-rococo architecture with the frescoed ceiling is stunning. Its organ was brought all the way from Mexico.

The town started out as an encomienda and later spread out to 148 barangays with around 50 families in each. In addition to the usual fishing and farming all over the province, Argao had industries like brickmaking. Among the men were a number of carpenters, bricklayers, blacksmiths, and silversmiths; the women engaged in weaving cloth made of indigenous materials and dressmaking. The town also boasts of its delicacies like its special torta (cake) and tuba (alcoholic beverage fermented from coconut juice). Chinese and Filipino traders from the other regions came to town to engage in business. By the late 19th century most of the townsfolk owned their own land.

The people of Argao were still generally loyal to the Spaniards, even as the towns nearer to the ciudad were pulsating with contained violence. This loyalty was simply a result of a general atmosphere of content as the town prospered on its own. It had ranked second or third among all the towns in the amount of tribute it paid to the Spanish government. The numerous industries invited so many Chinese and mestizo traders to do business there.

So there I could once more roam the beach at sunset as I did in Talisay without fear of being attacked by a stray rebel. I was surrounded by fishermen happy with their catch. When I visited the mountain barrios, I would see that the farmers were just as contented. Mainly this was because the farmers, who were natives, owned their lands and cultivated them themselves. There was therefore very much less power struggle here than in the friar haciendas or the encomiendas, where the indios were simply tenants. I prayed this prosperity would prevent the town from sympathizing with the revolutionary cause.

But there remained the sensitive issue of free labor demanded by the Spanish government. I, as parish priest, was put in charge of certifying illness or excuses which would exempt the natives from such tasks. Again, any human being vested with such power could abuse or exploit it, as I could have. But in many cases the people themselves invited this kind of abuse. They dangled all sorts of bribes under my nose.

"Padre, I cannot work at the road project over in that Barrio. The work is too heavy for me," a Chinese mestizo nicknamed Sitoy approached me at the parish office one day. "I have trouble with my stomach. Please grant me an exemption, Padre."

Sitoy looked like he was in his mid-forties, although I knew he was not more than thirty five years old. The man had aged prematurely due to his drinking habits. Now he had come to the convent with two pretty young women, Chinese mestizas with fine fair complexion and delicate features. Both women reeked of some exotic perfume which made me giddy and sick.

"What could be wrong with you, Sitoy? Is it too much of that *tubâ*? I see you all the time drinking with our buddies in your open veranda. I myself have sat with you. I know how drunk you can get, Sitoy," I told the man.

"Padre, if you grant me that exemption, my two sisters here will help you out at the convento. They can even stay with you there. They are good at a lot of things – cooking, needlework, choir, flower arrangements – and anything you would want them to do for you, Padre," Sitoy offered, with a conspiratorial note in his voice.

"Anything, just anything I would want them to do, Sitoy?" I answered with a little chuckle. "Why, how exciting it all sounds. But, Sitoy, I have seen enough of the devil. And there seems to be one grinning right behind you now, my friend. The only way to get rid of him is to work in that road project."

Sitoy looked confused. He obviously failed to comprehend how an aging man like me could refuse such a tempting offer – his two pretty sisters waiting on me hand and foot.

Surprisingly, the two young women looked crestfallen. They had been rejected. They had worked at looking their best for this interview. Their dresses looked like they were skillfully handmade and designed to display a lot of cleavage. I must say they looked tempting indeed! But I surprised myself by not being in the least stirred.

"*Muchas gracias, Hijas,*" I told the women. "But you would be better off working in one of those thriving industries in town. I know you are both very talented. You will meet a lot of those interesting gentlemen who come to town to look at your work."

The three lost siblings left abruptly with just an awkward word of goodbye.

There was a spirit of liberalism in this town. I knew that one of my predecessors, the parish priest twenty years before me, was well-loved by the people in spite of his long affair with a local woman with whom he had two children.

"Life here is too perfect," I realized. Life even became more interesting as I discovered the game of *Sabong* – two roosters fighting to the kill. My thorough enjoyment of the game matched the way I felt about bullfighting back in Spain - in the neightboring town of *Pamplona,* where the wild bulls were set free to run down the street on the feast of the patron saint, San Fermin.

But I knew that even this peace was bound to end soon, and I prayed that when the time came, I would be spared a violent death.

"Lord, Thy Will be done," I prayed with utter simplicity.

All this bliss was short lived. I came home late one evening and was startled by someone calling out to me in the dark. I cautiously approached the figure hiding behind a tree.

"Diego!" I exclaimed, careful to keep my voice down. Diego was the last person I expected to visit me here. What could have happened that was so urgent? My heart was beating wildly as I faced him.

As he emerged from hiding, I noticed that Diego's face looked haggard, as though he had not slept for days. He had dark circles under his eyes and lost a lot of weight.

"It won't be long now," he blurted out to me, struggling for breath.

"What is it, Diego? Please just relax," I consoled him, putting an arm over his shoulder. "Please remember - nothing that is of this world should matter too much. Everything here is transitory. It will all come to pass, Diego."

"I really should not be talking to you. I have betrayed my compadres by doing so. But I admire you deeply, Padre. I cannot allow you to die in the coming uprising," he said, gasping.

"Ah, yes, the uprising! I knew it was coming. So, what exactly is happening, Diego?" I asked.

"The rebels plan to go down to the towns and execute the parish priests and all Spanish leaders," Diego said, with a bit more calm. "Better start packing your belongings, Padre, and be sure to bring the ones of utmost value to you. Do not be surprised to find my carriage at your doorstep anytime from today. Go very quietly without telling anyone here as though you are just going on a regular errand."

"But, Diego, there was no need for you to come. Thank you for your kind offer. Señor Felix Suarez has already made arrangements for me to stay with them if the worst happens," I told him.

"You will be safe with the Suarez family in Naga. There you will be well protected by my men. Nobody will touch us sympathizers of the Katipunan."

On April 3, 1898, on Good Friday, as I was preparing for an early night, exhausted after the long procession, I was startled by a frantic knock on my door. A frightened assistant had come to break the news – a battle had been fought around the town of San Nicolas, in the street later named appropriately Calle Tres de Abril.

The following day, a messenger came to tell us that the *Katipuneros* had captured the towns of Toledo and Balamban right across the island of Cebu. On April 5, led by one Don Cornelio Miñoza, they attacked the town of Carcar, the next town south of Naga, and captured three Augustinian friars while two others escaped. The group then proceeded to Sibonga and captured the parish priest there. The *guardias civiles* had surrendered and some of them, being natives by birth, even joined the ranks of the *katipuneros*.

Then they proceeded to Argao apparently to capture me. They looked all over the town - in private houses, along the banks of the large river, and even in the [60] *sabongan* - but I might as well have fizzled into thin air.

Thus was I spared from torture and death. Fifteen days later, on April 20, 1898, seven men in Argao were executed by firing squad. The execution is believed to have been ordered by the friars.

Then, like a stroke of God's Divine Plan, the American fleet, led by US Navy Admiral George Dewey, defeated the Spanish army in the battle of Manila Bay on August 13, 1898. The bombing of the *USS Maine* in Havana, Cuba, on Feb. 14, 1898, had led the US to declare war against Spain and its colonies.

The city of Manila then fell into American hands, and the rest of the country followed. The Philippine revolutionary cause, disabled and defeated, found renewed hope in the hands of the Americans. The American occupation of the Philippine Islands was welcomed not by all but by many.

There was much celebration in the streets all over the country. The Spanish conquerors were finally gone! The widespread relief was pervasive.

---

[59] *a special cake made of eggs and coconut, in Binisaya*
[60] *the arena for fighting cocks, in Binisaya*

The Secret of Happiness is FREEDOM,

The Secret of Freedom is COURAGE.

-THUCYDIDES-

DISCUSSION VI
The Advocate

*"You seem to be going a lot to **Naga** these days," my son said.*

*"Yes, your aunt **Susan Torrefranca** introduced me to **Ermelinda Frias**, or 'Baby' for short", I told him. "She is a great grandchild of **Antolin Frias and Aleja Suarez**, his wife, and she works at the City Hall of Naga. She's really been very helpful. She gave me an entire family tree and pictures of the family. She's also been very generous with family folklore. I don't know what I would have done without her support."*

*"Baby's sister, **Mila Frias**, was also excited about the book. She has supplied her share of the folklore about Lolo Antolin. The great-grandfather loved to chase chickens around the yard for the slaughter. On a hot day, he could hardly wait to take off the heavy vestments immediately after ceremonies."*

"That can be interpreted to mean he threw convention to the winds in order to stay alive and do his work," he said.

"Or just plain realistic – in a day and time when everyone was drowned in idealism," I replied.

I wondered if the Padre's fondness for tuba, as Mila said, also addressed the issue of survival.

"Mila added that the town's prominent matrons adored him from below the pulpit as he preached, with his striking good looks, the enigmatic

eyes, the penchant for words. After the ceremonies, they would each hand him an envelope with contributions".

"*So he was a good fundraiser as well,*" *he said.*

"*These matrons also pushed their daughters to work for the church,*" *I said.*

"*No wonder he got two sisters pregnant,*" *he said.*

"*Then there is the gentleman,* **Rolando Frias***, the only surviving Suarez-Frias grandson and a look-alike of his grandfather in the picture. Uncle Roly can give a dramatic rendition of LA ULTIMO ADIOS in Spanish - Antolin Frias come alive as we imagine him preaching in the pulpit".*

"*This year, Baby and I went to see* **Mrs. Eugenia Chiong***. She graciously received us in her parlor overlooking the beach, making us feel very welcome. And she eagerly provided me with lots of memories of her childhood with her aunt,* **Aleja Suarez***, Antolin Frias's wife, and their two children,*" *I told him.* "*She described her aunt, Aleja, as warm and generous, an excellent homemaker who loved to cook rare and exquisite dishes. She was also nice, petite, charming and very hospitable, inviting everyone who came to visit to the food she had prepared. And she was outspoken and strict. She saw to it that the servants did everything just right.*"

"*So what was Aleja's family background?*" *he asked.*

"*Aleja was the daughter of* **Felix Suarez (1843)** *and* **Catalina Pañares Bartido***,*" *I answered.* "*Felix was a capitan of the town of Naga, Cebu at the time Father Antolin served as parish priest there. His wife, Catalina, was descended from the* **Duterte***'s, a prominent family of landowners and civic leaders mainly from* **Carcar, Cebu***. The Suarez's have been prominent citizens of the City of Naga and other parts of the Cebu province. Two of Aleja's brothers and several of her descendants have served as* **mayors of Naga** *up to the present day.*"

"*While he served as parish priest of Naga,*" *my son reflected.* "*Father Antolin would have been a close friend of the town's leading Suarez family. So, it is safe to presume that he was sheltered from the angry Katipuneros by the Suarez's in Naga in the insurrection of* **1898***, from where he eventually emerged as a layman, a lawyer, and married to their daughter* **Aleja***".*

*"Antolin and Aleja had two children," I said further, "a son, **Alfonso**, born in 1900, married to **Milagros Olmedo**, and a daughter, **Consuelo**, married to a lawyer, **Vicente Zacarias**. Together, Vicente Zacarias, and his father-in-law Antolin Frias fought legal battles and addressed legal issues as part of a team of other prominent lawyers of the early 1900's".*

"They must have been affluent and prominent in Naga," he said.

*"Not only in Naga but in the entire region. **Alfonso** was in the town council and in many church and civic organizations. His wife, **Milagros**, came from an affluent family in Baybay, Leyte. Alfonso was engaged in several business concerns, like mining and others," I said.*

"Did the Frias family live in Naga?" he asked.

*"Not really. Naga would have been too small for his large law practice. **Ms. Chiong** said that he was an attorney 'de campanilla', as prominent lawyers were referred to in those times. The Frias family lived in a large house on Sikatuna St., where the city's elite lived in those days."*

*"He sounds like an extraordinary man," my son said. "First, **a priest, then a lawyer**, and excellently fitting in into the perfect slot."*

*"He molded himself to the changes in society and what it asked of him" I said. "But, beneath it all must have been that desire to serve. First, there is always a strong desire. That and our thoughts have the power to make our wishes come true. We are then led into the right circumstances. In this case, **the American regime** had a pressing need for lawyers who knew the territory and the English language..."*

*"The lawyer, Frias, who as a friar once took charge of the large **friar estates of Talisay-Minglanilla**, would have been the legal expert in the massive land reform during the American regime. This, plus his knowledge of the English language, would have enhanced his services. Most of all, he was gifted with the talent and the intelligence to serve as advocate. We must not forget that he would have the personality and the ability for advocacy," I went on.*

"And are there some of his cases still on record?" my son asked.

*"Some of his cases at the **Supreme Court in Manila** can be found in google. One case, **THE UNITED STATES vs. GO SENG**, has him on record as a defense attorney of the defendant who was arrested on charges of drug use, which in those days meant opium," I replied.*

"The United States?" he asked.

"Yes, of course. This was in 1915. We were part of the United States until 1946, remember?" I replied.

"Geez, that's hard to imagine. And how did this case end?"

"Mr. Go Seng went to prison. How could the lawyer Frias win a drug use case against the United States?" I said. "But he at least tried."

"Anyway," I went on, "the other case on record is a civil case of the **Laureana Antonio** *family involving an inheritance issue, one side of the family against another. Antolin Frias is reflected as one of the many prominent attorneys involved in the case. One of the their lawyers is* **Vicente Zacarias***, his son-in-law".*

"But how and where did he prepare himself for such a career?" my son asked.

"There is no record of him attending the Colegio Seminario de San Carlos. Inquiries at the University of San Carlos records section revealed nothing. But the **University of Sto. Tomas** *has a record of his* **Bachiller en Artes degree in 1910***. I had to go to Manila to pick up a copy of his transcript," I told him, proud of my find. "But I have not found any degree in Civil Law. However, in the Supreme Court Law List his name appears as* **an attorney** *admitted to the Bar on* **March 30, 1911***".*

"Further inquiries revealed that lawyers in those days read the law or served as apprentices in law firms, then took the bar to qualify," I reported what I had been told.

"He then served as a lawyer with some prominence both in Cebu and in Manila. He held office in the area of the Cebu Metropolitan Cathedral, an aristocratic neighborhood in those days. Folklore speaks of him as an attorney de campanilla, *a lawyer of prominence."*

"Moreover, the **Journal of the Philippine Commision***, page 810, appointed Antolin frias 'to be* **auxiliary justice of the peace for the municipality of Cebu, Province of Cebu, Eleventh Judicial District, Section 1, Act. No. 2041'** **Thursday August 22, 1912***.*

"He had acquired rank in the legal profession" I finally said, reading from my notes.

"*He had taken the road a perfect warrior would take,*" my son reflected. "*And it made all the difference*".

"*His life always fell neatly into place,*" I told him.

"*So, how long did Padre Frias live? And what about his wife, Aleja?*" my son asked.

"*Lolo Frias* **died in 1925**. *He would have been* **66 years old** *then. There are no records of Aleja's birth. I was told she was already way into her twenties when she married Lolo Frias, maybe even thirty. That was in* **1898**," I replied.

"*Amazing...*"

ALFONSO SUAREZ FRIAS, son of Antolin Frias y Ramos
and Aleja Suarez
1900 - 1963

Photo Courtesy of Ermelinda Frias

Sons of Alfonso Suarez Frias and Milagros Olmedo Frias
Standing from L to R - Alfonso II, Ruben, Vicente, Antolin.
Seated L to R - Rogelio, Fernando

CONSUELO FRIAS ZACARIAS

(- 1988), first child of Antolin Frias and Aleja Suarez Photo
courtesy of Ermelinda Frias Lee

CONSUELO FRIAS ZACARIAS (SEATED MIDDLE)
WITH CHILDREN AND GRANDCHILDREN

Photo courtesy of Ermelinda Frias Lee

VICENTE OLMEDO FRIAS
former executive judge
of Iloilo

ERMELINDA (BABY) FRIAS,
granddaughter of
Alfonso Suarez Frias and
Milagros Olmedo Frias
2014

Photo Courtesy of Ermelinda Frias Lee

Great-grandchildren of FR. ANTOLIN FRIAS and ALEJA SUAREZ
Naga, Cebu

Photo Courtesy of Ermelinda Frias Lee

SUAREZ-FRIAS CLAN, Naga, Cebu

Student records of FR. ANTOLIN FRIAS Y RAMOS from the UNIVERSITY OF STO. TOMAS where he pursued a BACHILLER DE ARTES in 1910 (page 1)

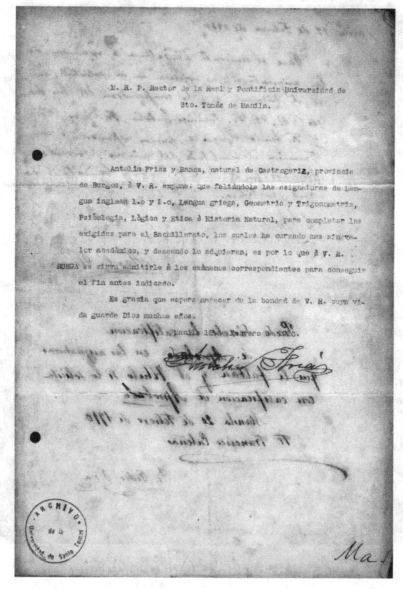

Certifico: Que D. Antolín Frías y Ramos, natural de Castrogeriz, provincia de Burgos, aprobado de ingreso, en el distrito de Burgos en el curso académico de 1869 á 1870 se matriculó en las asignaturas de Gramática latina y castellana 1.º curso y obtuvo en los exámenes ordinarios la calificación de Aprobado, matriculado en el de 1870 á 1871 en las de Gramática latina y castellana 2.º curso, Geografía, Historia de España é Historia Universal, obtuvo en los ordinarios la calificación de Aprobado en todas y premio en la tercera; matriculado en el Instituto de Valladolid en el curso de 1871 á 1872 en las de Retórica y Poética, Física y Química y Aritmética y Álgebra, obtuvo en los ordinarios las calificaciones de Notablemente Aprovechado y accesit en las dos primeras y Aprobado en las dos últimas en el curso de 1874 á 1875, examinado en esta Universidad de las de Lengua inglesa, 1.º y 2.º cursos, Psicología, Lógica y Ética, Geometría y Trigonometría, Lengua griega é Historia natural, obtuvo la calificación de Aprobado en todas

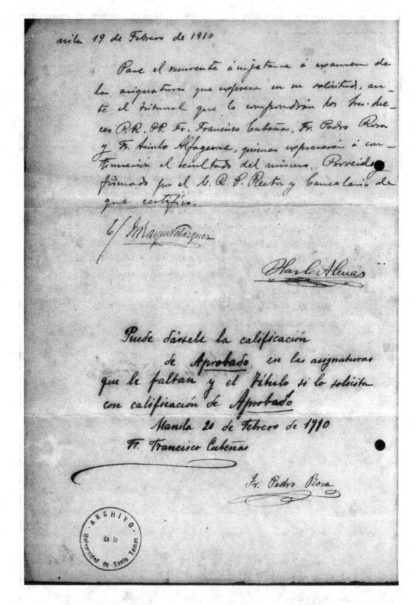

Copied with permission from the archives of University of Sto. Tomas, Manila, Philippines 2014

Below is a clear typewritten copy of the student records in Spanish:

M.R.P. Rector de la Real y Pontificia Universidad de Sto. Tomas de Manila

Antolin Frias y Ramos, natural de Castrogeriz, Provincia de Burgos, a V.R. expone:

Que faltandole las asignaturas de Lengua Inglesa 1.0 y 2.0, Lengua Griega, Geometria y Trigonometria, Psicologia, Logica y Etica, y Historia Natural, para completa las exigidas para el Bachillerato, los cuales ha cursado mas sin valor academico, y deseando lo adquieren; es por lo que a V.R. RUEGA se sirva adminitirle a los examenes correspondientes para conseguir el fin antes indicado.

Es gracia que espera merecer de la bondad de V.R. cuya vida guarde Dios muchos años.

Manila, 18 Febrero de 1910
(sgd.) Antolin Frias

Certifico: Que D. Antolin Frias y Ramos, natural de Castrogeriz, provincial de Burgos, aprobado de ingreso en el Instituto de Burgos en el curso academica de 1869 a 1870 se matriculo en las asignaturas de Gramatica Latin y Castellana, curso yabinos en los examines ordinario los calificaciones de aprobado, matriculado en el de 1870 a 1871 en los Grammatica Latin y Castellana 2.0, Geografia, Historia de España, Historia Universal, obtuvo en los ordinarios de certificacion de Aprobado en todas y permiso en la tercera, matriculado en el Instituto de Valladolid en el curso de 1871 a 1872 en las de Retorica Poetica, Fisica y Insiencia y Algebra, obliver en los ordinaries calificaciones de Notablewen, te abrobediado y en las provincias y aprobado en los dos en el curso de 1874-1875; exminado de los Lengua Inglesa 1 y 2, cursos Psilogia, Logica y Etica, Geometria, Lengua Griega y Historia natural, Obtuvo la calificacion de Aprobado en todos.

Manila, 19 de Febrero de 1910

Pasé a Tribunal de los asignaturas que expresa en solicitud, ante el Tribunal que lo aprobados, Fr. Cubenas, Fr. Francisco, Fr. Pedro Rosa, Fr. Asito Alfagena,

(Signed) M. Velasquez

Puede Lansele la calificacion de Aprobado en las asignaturas que le faltan y el Titulos si lo solicita con calification de Aprobado.
Manila 20 de Febrero de 1910
Fr. Francisco Cubenas
(Sgd.) Fr. Pedro Rosa

Student Records of Antolin Frias at the University of Sto. Tomas, Manila

(ENGLISH TRANSLATION)

M.R.P. Rector of the Royal and Pontifical University of Sto. Tomas, Manila

I, Antolin Frias y Ramos, native of Castrogeriz, province of Burgos, state: That I lack the missing subjects: English Language 1 and 2, Greek Language, Geometry and Trigonometry, Psychology, Logic and Ethics, and Natural History to complete the requirements for the Baccalaureate, and that I be allowed to take the corresponding examinations for the purpose indicated above.

May your kindness be awarded with Grace and may God grant you many years.

(sgd.) Antolin Frias

I certify: That Antolin Frias y Ramos, native of Castrogeriz, province of Burgos, attended an institute in Burgos in the academic course 1869-1870 in the subjects of Latin and Spanish Grammar; in 1870-1871 in the Latin and Spanish Grammar 2, Geography, History of Spain, Universal history, obtaining an approved certificate for all courses; in the third year, enrolled at the institute in Valladolid in 1871-1872 in Rhetoric, Poetics, Physical Science, Algebra, and passed with notable marks. In 1874-1875, he enrolled in English 1, Psychology 1 and 2, Logic and Ethics, Geometry, Greek Language, and Natural history, and passed all courses.

Manila, February 19, 1910 (sgd) M. Velasquez

Endorse to the Tribunal this request to take the qualifying examinations of the subjects mentioned in this request, as approved by Fr. Francisco

Cubenas, Fr. Pedro Rosa, Fr. Asito Alfagena, and the results to be approved by the R.P. Rector and Chancellor of the desired certificate.

(signed) M. Velasquez

The missing subjects can be approved as Passed, and the Title can be granted.

Manila, February 20, 1910

Friar Francisco Cubenas

(Sgd) Fr. Pedro Rosa

(Translated by the Author)

Republic of the Philippines
SUPREME COURT
Manila

EN BANC

G.R. No. L-10397 August 3, 1915

THE UNITED STATES, *Plaintiff-Appellee*,
vs. GO SENG, *Defendant-Appellant*.

Antolin Frias for appellant.
Acting Attorney-General Zaragoza for appellee.

JOHNSON, *J*.:

This defendant was charged with a violation of the Opium Law. The complaint alleged "that on or about December 24, 1913, within the municipal limits of the municipality of Cebu, of this province and judicial district, the said Go Seng, being in no manner authorized by law, did willfully, unlawfully, and criminally smoke, chew, swallow, and inhale opium, thus incurring the risk of becoming a recidivist; with violation of the law."

After hearing the evidence, the honorable Cayetano Lukban, auxiliary judge of the Court of First Instance of the Twentieth District, found the defendant guilty of the crime charged and sentenced him to pay a fine of P350 and costs, and to suffer subsidiary imprisonment in case of insolvency.

From that sentence the defendant appealed to this court. A question of fact only is presented by the appellant.

From an examination of the evidence, we find that two witnesses, whose credibility has not been impeached in the slightest degree, swore positively that they caught the defendant in the act of smoking opium. The pipe used and the opium which was found in the possession of the accused were presented as proof during the trial of the cause. In addition to that proof, we find from an exhibit presented during the trial of the cause that the defendant had heretofore been accused and found guilty of a violation of the Opium Law, and had been sentenced, on the 29th day of September, 1910, to pay a fine of P350.

The Attorney-General, in view of the fact that the defendant had been once before convicted of the same crime, recommends that the sentence of the lower court be modified, and that in addition to the fine imposed by the lower court, a sentence of imprisonment for a period of three months be also imposed.

With the recommendation we are inclined to agree. We think, in view of the fact that the defendant has been found guilty of a violation of the Opium Law twice, that the penalty to be imposed for the second offense should be more severe than that which was imposed for the first offense. (See U.S. *vs.* Lim Sing, 23 Phil. Rep., 424.)

Therefore, the sentence of the lower court is hereby modified and it is hereby ordered and decreed that the defendant be sentenced to be imprisoned for a period of three months and to pay a fine of P350 and the costs, and in case of insolvency to suffer subsidiary imprisonment in accordance with the provisions of the law. So ordered.

Arellano, C.J., Torres, Carson, Trent,
and Araullo, JJ., concur.

www.chanrobles.com/scdicision/juresprundence/1915/gr 1-10397-1915.php

Republic of the Philippines
SUPREME COURT
Manila

EN BANC

G.R. No. L-22399 December 12, 1924

In the matter of the will of Laureana Antonio, deceased. MARIANO ANTONIO, petitioner-appellant,
vs.
SANTIAGO ANTONIO, ET AL., opponents-appellees, and JORGE R. NERI, ET AL., opponents-appellants.

Vicente Zacarias, Antolin Frias, Del Rosario and Del Rosario, McVean and Vickers, and Camus and Delgado for petitioner-appellant.
No appearance for opponents-appellants.
Fisher, DeWitt, Perkins and Brady, Araneta and Zaragoza, Paredes, Buencamino and Yulo, and Palma, Leuterio and Yamson for opponents-appellees.

AVANCEÑA, *J.:*

This is a proceeding for the probate of the will of Laureana Antonio. *lawphil.net* The lower court denied the probate of this will on the ground that it was not executed with the solemnities prescribed by the law.

The will in question consists of seven pages actually used. It is not denied that its first six pages are in accordance with the law, but there is a dispute as to the last page 7. In this page the will ends, and at the bottom thereof there appear the signatures of the testator and the three witnesses to the will, after which comes the attestation clause signed also at the bottom by the three witnesses. No signature whatever appears on either margin of this page, and the lower court denied the probate of the will on account of the testator and the three subscribing witnesses not having signed on the left margin.

The decision of this court in the case of *Abangan vs. Abangan* (40 Phil., 476), is square in point. In that case the will had but two pages. The first contained entirely the whole text of the will, and the second contained the last part of the attestation clause. The first page was signed by the testator at the bottom of the text of the will with the three attesting witnesses, and the second was also signed at the bottom of the attestation clause by the three witnesses. In none of said pages was there any signature on either margin. In that case this court held that the will should be admitted to probate. On principle there is no difference between the instant, and the Abangan case. If there is any, as in fact there is, as to certain details, it is in favor of the probate of the will in the instant case. It must not be forgotten that the object of the law in prescribing certain solemnities for the execution of wills is to insure and safeguard their authenticity, and consequently the courts, in deciding the various cases that may present themselves on this matter, must not lose sight of this object of the law. In the instant case, as above indicated, the attesting witnesses signed twice on the last page of the will of Laureana Antonio, while in the Abangan case the witnesses signed only once in each of its two pages. So that the only possible objection to this page of the will of Laureana Antonio is that it was not signed on the left margin by the testator and the three attesting witnesses, it having been signed only at the bottom of the text of the will and the attestation clause. This is exactly the rule laid down in the Abangan case to the effect that under such circumstances the absence of the signatures of the testator and the attesting witnesses from the left margin is not such a defect as would justify the denial of its probate.

The judgment appealed from is reversed, and the will of Laureana Antonio admitted to probate, without special findings as to costs. So ordered.

Johnson, Street, Malcolm, Villamor, Ostrand, Johns, and Romualdez, JJ., concur.

http://www.lawphil.net/judjuris/juri1924/dec1924/gr_l-22399_1924.html

CHAPTER 23

THE HAPPY FAMILY

Naga, 1905

On fine afternoons, before the sun set, peals of laughter echoed through the beach in the poblacion of Naga. The happy sound blended with the raucous of the birds as they settled for the night in the Magtalisay trees lining the shore.

At the beach, a couple walked barefoot on the sand, the man holding a little boy of about four in one hand, and the woman holding the hand of a little girl of six. The man was of average height but his build was sturdy, his strong muscles straining against the thin white cotton shirt. He looked like he had just turned forty years old. She was about thirty years old, small and petite, looking very appealing in her long cotton skirt and sheer kimono blouse. In contrast to the man, who clearly had the face of a Caucasian, she had the Malayan features of a native. A closer look at her face, though, would reveal eyes unusually bright with laughter and lips pursed like she was forever waiting to be kissed.

This was how we would have appeared to anyone who cared to look – man, woman, children - set against infinity.

A perfect portrait!

"Alfonso, *Hijo*," I would call out to my little boy, who wandered off too far, "Not too close to the water, please!" The boy only ran faster and farther away from me. He was a fearless little fellow who enjoyed meeting the waves head on and running away before they crashed and washed him out to sea.

The woman, his mother, would laugh at the boy's antics, and soon I and the boy were both teasing the waves. The little girl squealed with delight and clapped her hands. For a few precious moments, the world revolved around the four happy people, united as one in their delight with the sea, the fiery sky, the birds, and each other – harmony, happiness.

"What have I done to deserve this peace?" I would think, as dusk descended and a profound silence wrapped itself around us. The birds had fallen asleep and the gentle lapping of waves had turned into a lullaby.

Twilight – this had always been my time of the day. This was when the significant events in my life happened. This was the moment things clicked into place like the pieces of a jigsaw puzzle finally done.

[61]"*Buenas noches*, Padre," people would greet me as I walked back home with my family – wife, son, and daughter.

"*Buenas noches*," I would reply, my voice still ringing with pleasure from the afternoon's events.

I wished people would stop calling me "Padre". After all, I was now a married man with two children. But my new social status did not seem to make a difference to the community here. To the people who knew me long, I would always be a priest.

But, to be honest, no matter what anyone thought, this was the plain truth. I would always be a priest, indelibly marked with the sacrament of Holy Orders. Now, though, I had officially left the Augustinian Order and was no longer bound to my priestly duties.

Am I dreaming all this? Are you wondering whether I am languishing in some jail and having these hallucinations? No, to be honest, I emerged from the turbulent years of the Revolution a married man.

I married Aleja Suarez and in that same year, our daughter, Consuelo, was born, followed by our son Alfonso in 1900. We have lived in the Suarez Residence in Naga all these years.

One night, after dinner, while Aleja was tidying up and getting the children ready for bed, I took my usual seat in the large veranda facing the sea. Many years ago, it was in this very spot in the Suarez family home that I and Aleja had our first private conversation and our friendship began.

It was in this very house where, as parish priest of Naga, I was warmly welcomed by the entire Suarez family. Here I had finally found the home I sorely needed. And inevitably it was in this house where I had taken refuge from the Katipuneros in 1898. My very life was in danger then and here I had stayed for a few months until the rebels had surrendered.

I spent those months in forced "exile" from my ministry, and I wandered about the Suarez house dazed, confused, and bewildered as the world revolved around me in complete chaos. The uncertainty of the colony's fate and that of my life weighed down on my Spirit. I spent my days sitting at the veranda, staring out into the sea in absolute silence.

"Do not bother the Padre," I would hear Señora Suarez telling her family and everyone in her household, "what he needs now is peace and quiet."

It was Aleja who would bring me my meals, very special dishes which she had herself cooked. The cakes made of [62] *cassava* offered me some comfort.

"Do you mind if I sit with you?" she would ask me in a meek voice, "I promise I won't say a word."

I could only manage a nod and a weak smile. So she would sit and watch me eat each morsel, as a mother would a small child. Her glorious dishes saved me from complete dissolution. It became the only pleasure I was capable of feeling in those dark days.

"You have not finished the soup. This pumpkin in coconut milk is just what you need. You have lost so much weight, Padre," she would push me on.

Gradually, I began warming up to her. Her simplicity, her sincerity, her innocence proved to be the needed medicine. We began to have long serious conversations.

When the Spaniards surrendered to the Americans in December of that year, I and Aleja had already agreed to get married. Since I was a priest, we could only seal our vows with the civil registrar of the new American regine.

The town of Naga had always been sympathetic to the American presence. The 73rd Infantry Battalion of the US Army held camp at the old Corro residence in the town.

I enjoyed spending time with the American soldiers. They obviously needed a minister who spoke their language. They, too, like the Spaniards before them, found themselves in totally strange territory where life was uncertain and unpredictable. They, too, had left their families back home. They, too, were extremely lonely.

Many of the Americans were Protestants. I just knew at that point that the American presence would bring the Protestant sects in our midst soon. But I had faith that we were all Christians and should just co-exist as believers of Christ.

So I would visit the camp regularly and talk to the men in the English I had learned in school. Thus, as a self-appointed minister, I began to feel needed once more. The work in addition to my harmonious home life enabled me to heal. I felt that a new mission lay ahead of me and I would once again be of service to others.

At the seminary in Valladolid, two semesters of English were required for graduation. And now my mastery of Latin facilitated learning more English, which was necessary for me to enter into any of the professions under this new regime.

I was truly just a microcosm in a macrocosm. Both my little world and the world at large were simultaneously undergoing a metamorphosis. It was too early to determine what the next day would bring.

---

[61] *good evening, in Spanish*
[62] *A special cake made of cassava roo*

CHAPTER 24

RENEWED HOPE - THE AMERICAN REGIME

Not long after the uncertain period of several years in which I peacefully floated around in Naga, among my newfound family and the new society, I finally found a new calling and a deeper purpose.

By an Act of Congress of the United States, the American Government of the Philippine Islands had purchased the friar haciendas in the Philippines – in the provinces of Laguna, Bulacan, Cavite, Bataan, Cebu, Rizal, Isabella, and Mindoro – all 164,127 hectares of it – from four original corporate owners. One of them was the Recoletos Order of the Philippine Islands, a branch of the Order of Saint Augustine in which I used to belong. Before the purchase was finalized, the lands had to be resurveyed and reassessed and the titles and deeds reviewed.

Having been the administrator of the eight-thousand hectare Talisay-Minglanilla friar haciendas, originally owned by the Recoletos Order of the Philippine Islands, I was the person who knew the area like the palm of my hand. The Order itself had asked my help in reviewing the perimeters and other features of the lands. I had also related with the tenants long enough to deal with them like a friend. And a great help was my mastery of the native language, *Binisaya*.

My biggest task was to identify the tenants and certify that they had been working on their land for a certain period. The tenants, who for many years had been working for the friar Orders of the Augustinians and the Recoletos, had known me for almost thirty years. Their children, now grown, were mere babies when I started taking charge of their lands – inspecting the conditions, reminding them of their dues, solving problems, chasing their chickens for a free roasted meal, drinking their tuba delightfully.

The original tenants or occupants were given an option to lease the property for a reasonable sum, but not more than a period of three years. The other option would be to purchase the property at easy installments. An individual was allowed to buy utmost 144 hectares and a corporation 1,024 hectares.

Sidro, now a bent old man, soon knocked on my door at the Suarez ancestral home in Naga. The two of us - one a former friar landlord and the other the humble tenant from a totally bygone era - held each other very long in a tight embrace, like two brothers reunited after a long war. Then we sat together in utter silence, each waiting for the other's tears to subside.

"I think I know why you're here, Sidro," I finally said. "As an old settler of the land you've occupied, you are now required to either lease or purchase it from the US administration."

Sidro merely grunted. He seemed too overcome with emotion to say a word.

"So, which one is it, Sidro? Are you leasing or buying?" I prodded him on.

Sidro remained tongue-tied.

"Ah, Sidro, let me guess," I said further, "you can neither afford to lease or purchase the land."

Sidro nodded his head sadly. He continued nodding until he finally cried out in violent sobs.

"We have no money, Padre. Ah, can I still call you 'padre'? Okay, if we refuse to lease or purchase the land, it will be confiscated from us, and we will have to leave," the old man finally blurted out between sobs.

"But the installment terms of the purchase are so easy. I believe you have fifteen years to pay in equal annual installments at only a little interest – 4 per cent each year, or am I wrong? Then, you and your family will be the bona fide owners of your land. Just think of it, Sidro. This American administration certainly has its humane side. Would you have preferred being just a tenant for the friars?" I consoled the old man. But Sidro had lost his voice.

"Alright, Sidro," I continued, "I'll find a way to help you and people like you. Just stay where you are and wait for news from me."

Soon after, other former tenants like Sidro were knocking on my door. They brought a lot of tribute – sacks of rice, fruits, vegetables, and best of all, to my absolute delight, *tuba* and the chickens. I realized there was little money being circulated in these times and bartering of goods served as the currency of exchange.

I eventually found an easy solution to the tenants' financial dilemma. My hands were soon occupied with the formation of cooperatives. Organized in coops, the tenants all over the haciendas could now pull their resources together to purchase the lands from the new US administration.

To achieve this goal, I had to employ lawyers. This led me to make a momentous decision – to become a lawyer myself.

This was the year 1908. My son, Alfonso, was eight years old, while Consuelo was ten. Aleja had been a loving and competent wife and mother. My parents-in-laws, Felix and Catalina Suarez, had been very supportive. This sturdy home environment had given me the confidence to embark on a new career. I decided to study for the law at the University of Santo Tomas in Manila.

Aleja was ecstatic when she heard of my plans. She encouraged me strongly, assuring me that she and her family were perfectly capable of taking care of themselves and the children in my absence. She was just her typical unselfish self as she prodded me on.

"Just think of it, Amor. Me on a big boat! Me strolling on the Escolta, shopping for beautiful clothes, exquisite jewelry! Me, the lawyer's wife," she would repeatedly exclaim, pretending to be selfish, pretending to be excited. But I knew she was only thinking of me and sparing me from guilt and doubt. I knew she would miss me terribly, especially for our walks at twilight.

And I would miss her. But I also knew she would always be there, like the Evening Star.

So I went ahead and pursued a *Bachiller en Artes* degree at the University of Santo Tomas, ready for all it took. And luck was on my side. The administrators of the university, all friars of the Dominican order, knowing me as a former Augustinian, credited the collegiate units I had taken at the *Colegio Seminario* in *Valladolid*.

I took and passed the qualifying examinations on these required subjects, then proceeded to read on the ones I had not taken, like Psychology and the Sciences, and passed these, as well. Thus I was granted a *Bachiller en Artes* degree from the University of Santo Tomas in 1910.

Meanwhile, while studying, I had been working as an apprentice in several big law firms both in Manila and in Cebu in order to prepare for the bar exams. My connections to some prestigious lawyers of that time had made it easy for me to acquire the knowledge and experience to pass the bar.

I became a bona fide lawyer in 1914, and practiced law both in Cebu and in Manila. I held office in the city of Cebu, located in the shadow of the Cebu Cathedral. Most of my cases were land disputes among heirs, especially those which involved the former friar estates, in which I was the expert.

It was not long before the Chinese community in the city heard about me and my services. One morning, I found some Chinese folk waiting for me in my office. They introduced themselves as the family of Go Seng.

"My husband, Go Seng, has been in jail for two years now, Mr. Frias," the older lady in the group managed to say through her tears. "He was caught using opium and convicted in the lower court."

"I am so sorry for you, Mrs. Go. But what can I do to help you?" I asked her gently in Binisaya.

"We would like to appeal his case to the higher court," she told me between sobs.

"You mean, the Supreme Court," I clarified. "But, tell me, Mrs. Go. Do you really believe your husband is innocent? Don't you think he deserves his penalty?"

"Please, Mr. Frias, try to understand. My husband has been using opium since he was a young boy, before these Americans ran the country. He was suffering from so much pain, you see. The opium relieved his pain," she said, sobbing even louder at the memory of her husband's suffering.

"What is wrong with him?" I asked.

"He has severe pains here," she said, touching her lower back, "and this is a result of carrying heavy loads as he was growing up. You see, he worked in a cargo boat which carried lumber from Mindanao. This was the only way he could feed his poor and ailing parents and grandparents."

I flinched at the idea of a mere boy carrying loads of lumber and travelling long distances on rough seas. The heaviest load I had carried as a boy was a horse's harness. I had not forgotten the poor and miserable conditions around the Chinese community during the Spanish regime, at the time I was parish priest of San Nicolas.

"Can you find a doctor who can certify on his disability?" I asked the woman.

"You know good doctors are hard to find, Mr. Frias. Not one of those we consulted even knows about his problem," she shook her head as she spoke.

I could easily understand what she was saying. With the limited equipment, it would be difficult to diagnose such old scars deep inside the body. A broken bone would reveal itself in an x-ray, which was readily available. But I felt that Mr. Go Seng's injury was more of the musculature or the nerves along the spine.

I had seen enough sick pilgrims in Castrogeriz to understand the nature of such injuries. Many instances, these pilgrims went back home permanently scarred from their long difficult walk on the Camino de Santiago.

"Okay, I will take your case, Mrs. Go," I finally told the sobbing lady.

So, I, Antolin Frias y Ramos, the lawyer, soon found himself in the Supreme Court in Manila, handling a criminal case as the defense lawyer of Mr. Go Seng, defending my client against the plaintiff, the United States of America. But my efforts were in vain. Drug use was strictly prohibited under this American administration. Mr. Go Seng finally served a jail sentence.

CHAPTER 25

PARADISE REGAINED

1922. My family –Aleja, Consuelo, and Alfonso, and I had been living right in the city of Cebu at Sikatuna St., an affluent residential district just off the commercial district of T. Padilla St. We had moved here from the ancestral home in Naga ever since I established my law firm near the cathedral, just a short ride away. This move had also proven convenient for the children to attend nearby schools – Alfonso at the Colegio Seminario de San Carlos and Consuelo at a convent school for girls.

Alfonso, now a young man of 20, had finished his college studies at the Colegio de San Carlos and was working with a business firm. He had shown interest in a nice young woman, Milagros, and it was only a matter of time before the two tied the knot. Milagros came from a nice, affluent, landed family in Leyte, and she had been well-educated with the nuns at the Colegio de la Inmaculada Conception. Aleja and I were happy to welcome her into our family.

Consuelo, now 22, had been married to one of my partners, a young promising lawyer named Vicente Zacarias. The couple lived in a beautiful house near our law office.

With our children settled, Aleja and I felt fulfilled and immensely at peace with our lives. Our house was a haven where relatives from Naga frequently visited whenever they came to the city.

"Come, eat some of these, have a taste of that, please come!" Aleja would exclaim happily whenever anyone came. "I have just made some *paellas* and *tortas*. And there are different kinds of *dulces*, new recipes which I have just learned from our cooking sessions with Doña Mercedes."

That was our home, a popular destination for visiting relatives from Naga and elsewhere, where a sumptuous feast perrenially awaited them on the dining table.

Yet there were days when I would sit alone in my balcony and gaze at the stars, listening to my heart telling me that there were matters left unsettled in my life. Something always tugged at my insides at times when I least expected it, but it was a matter which had remained buried way deep below my conscious mind. I could not give it a name. Now as age crept in, I felt the pressing need to look at it in the eye and wrestle with it.

Then, one day, I finally encountered the very person who would put me at rest.

I had just spent a hectic morning at the Municipio in Talisay, clearing up papers from my latest case – a will contestation between two brothers –particularly demanding for an older man like me. It was time for me to go slow. Starving, I could hardly wait to have lunch at an outdoor carenderia by the beach.

Just as I walked by one of the offices, I heard a woman's voice through an open doorway. Was it the agitation in her voice that stopped me in my tracks? Or was it because she sounded like someone I knew well from another time?

"Fidelina", she was saying, with a note of impatience in her voice, "it is spelled f-i-d-e-l-i-n-a. It is not f-e-d-i-...Why is it so difficult for you? I have spelled my name out to you so many times already. Now, may I repeat for one last time...Fidelina Bascon Regner!"

"Juan," I called out to the male clerk, "her name is spelled f-i-d-e-l-i-n-a. Please pay more attention, *Hijo*."

The woman turned towards me and gave a visible start. She was flushed with surprise. All at once I knew who she was. Tired and hungry, I felt faint with the emotion welling up inside me at the sight of her. It took all my strength to remain standing. I felt like one who finally meets the person one has missed for a very long time.

"Thank you," the woman mumbled below her breath.

"Fidelina," I uttered her name like we had known each other a long time. An awkward silence followed. I realized she was stunned with disbelief.

"Fidelina," I said again, this time offering my hand. She stood and took my hand like someone dazed. I held her hand with both of mine. Our hands and our eyes locked for a few eternal seconds.

"Fidelina," I repeated. "It is so good to see you again. How you've grown! I've been thinking about you all this time."

She remained quiet and gave a faint smile, her mouth twitching nervously at the corners, her eyes large with shock. I did not realize I was still holding her hand in mine, and it had turned cold and clammy. I let it go, then she held both her hands clasped against her breast, like someone imploring for mercy.

"You must be hungry. Come and have lunch with me, then we'll both come back here and deal with your business."

"I just wanted to have some documents done on a property which my husband and I have just acquired," she managed to blurt out.

"Your husband? So you are now a married woman? Come, do tell me about it over a hot lunch," I heard myself say.

We, the older man and the young woman, elicited stares around us as we sat across each other in one corner of the cafeteria, with our food laid out – rice, roast pork, chicken soup, *arroz caldo, caldereta.* We both sat without saying a word. Words suddenly became superfluous and redundant.

But the silence between us turned strangely comfortable. In between bites, I studied her face which very closely resembled mine. She was wearing a simple dress of white cotton muslin, with lace around the neckline and sleeves, very elegant.

"Fidelina, we are going to have fresh pineapple for dessert" I announced, like a father would make a choice for his little girl. The familiarity was quite spontaneous.

"Now, tell me all about you, your life, your family", I asked her.

"Nothing much to tell, actually. I am married to a wonderful man, Loselo Regner. He works as an engineer with the Philippine National Railway. We live a few blocks from the main station in the Ciudad. We have eight children at the moment," she said, with obvious effort to keep her voice steady.

"At the moment! You mean, that isn't enough! But that's a lot of children! How are they, and what are their names?" I asked her.

She enumerated her children's names – Luis, Rafaela, Epifania, Antolin, Sebastian, Leo, Lorenzo, Andrea.

"Ah, so you have named one of them after me!" I exclaimed delightfully, with a smile.

"And if I have another girl, I will surely name her Nicolasa," she said, eyeing me more closely.

"Ahhh…" I sighed, not knowing what to say next. She leaned back, searching my face.

"So how is she, your mother?" I finally found the words.

I was so sure it was the question she was waiting for, which she was afraid I would not have the nerve to ask.

I am sure you broke her heart terribly at one point. But you see she is so amazing that she moved on and led a happy life – much to your advantage… I could almost hear her thoughts.

Yes, my heart was split in half as well. I see you have moved on too. And here you are—my daughter – a good person leading a happy, productive life – I am so proud of you —all our suffering was not futile – I prayed she would read my mind and decipher the words I did not have the nerve to say out loud.

"She is happy and healthy," she instead replied with obvious pride in her voice, "She has been living in Manila with my half-sister Corazon and her husband, a Chinese businessman. They are all doing business and thriving well in that big city."

A thoughtful silence followed her revelation. I felt that I should explain to her the circumstances surrounding her birth, but refrained from saying a word. No one could ever put oneself in another man's shoes, and no words seemed adequate to express another man's feelings. Instead I looked directly into her eyes and tried to look happy for Nicolasa.

"Juan, Corazon's father, left the family to return to Mexico when we were children," she went on, this time answering the question which I dared not ask. "Mama Asay received plenty of support from her parents and the Bascon family here in Talisay, with the sugar lands and all."

I remembered how the friar lands were settled in the American Regime. As old tenants, the Bascons in Dumlog would have turned out purchasing the land they occupied. They were good tenants in my time, and I was happy for them.

"So, don't you sometimes wish that you could also live in Manila, if you didn't have such a large family?" I asked her.

"No, not by all means!" she exclaimed, "My life is fulfilled right here. Loselo is a loving husband, hardworking, generous, quiet."

"Quiet?" I teased. "Is that good?"

"Well, yes, because I happen to have a hot temper. And when I am annoyed, I make a lot of noise," she said with a trace of laughter in her voice. "We love each other very much. What more can a woman want? And also my mother has put me in charge of her landholdings here in Talisay, which she claims someday I and Corazon will inherit. Loselo and I have also been acquiring more lands here for our numerous children to inherit someday."

She sounded so resolute, so self-assured, and with that hot temper – how very like my mother. How Fidelina reminded me of Luisa, my mother, with her temperament and her thick curly mass of black hair. I remembered my mother's hair spread out when she unknotted it at bedtime - a thick mass in which I, as a boy, loved to bury my face and breathe in the sweet aroma of sweat and palm oil.

"And your aunt Eustaquia and Apolonio - how are they?" I finally dared to ask her the question which had long festered in my mind.

Fidelina gave a deep sigh, like she was glad that I at least remembered these two people whose lives I had touched so profoundly.

"Tia Yayang is happy and healthy, thank God. She has opened an embroidery shop and does [63] *barong tagalogs, kimonas, patadyongs* and pretty children's dresses. But Tio Dodong has a problem with his heart. Besides Jose, they had many more children, among them Carmen, Pastor, Rita, Presentacion, and triplets who died in childbirth," she informed me.

I digested the news quietly with downcast eyes and knitted brows, as though struggling with an idea. Jose – Jose, my son?

But, I was happy to hear that Yayang and Dodong's marriage turned out to be fruitful, with many children of their own.

"Do you see them often – their children, your cousins?" I asked her, my heart beating fast.

"Yes, I see them around, but it is Jose whom I see often. He comes to my house every Sunday to have lunch with my family," she answered, then after a little pause, said, "it is so strange how he resembles you so closely. He looks like he could be your son."

I felt myself stiffen but just as soon composed myself. For a moment we were surrounded by a thick silence. She knew the truth about Jose's paternity.

"Well, you two are cousins and I am so glad to hear that you are looking out for each other," was all I could manage to say.

"Oh yes, I do take care of my own, and Jose is one of them," she told me with unmistakable kindness in her voice. *He is my half-brother and your son,* I could feel the reproach in her mind. I wanted to tell her I could not acknowledge Jose openly out of respect for the man who heroically claimed him to be his son – Dodong de la Cerna.

"Ah, *Hija,*" I said instead. "All these years and I have not given you anything. Will you ever forgive me?"

"Oh, please, don't even think of it," she consoled me. "God has been kind to all of us, to me and to you and everyone else our lives have touched."

"But wait," she blurted out, her voice excited, "you have left me with something. These eyes – they come from you – this rare light brown-green color, the way they come alive with your thoughts and emotions. *And yes, because of them, people have called me 'señora'. Señora Peding.*"

I who was so good with words was at a loss for words. For the next few moments, we were both very quiet.

"Well, we must be getting back now, so you'll get those documents done before the train to the ciudad leaves without you. You are taking the train, aren't you?" I said instead.

Then my voice broke as I choked back the tears.

"Oh yes, my husband Selo will be working on this train this afternoon," she replied with pride, pretending not to notice.

As we stood up to leave, I held my arms out to my daughter. She came closer and gave me a hug.

"Hija, hija," I finally said with a burst of tenderness, "Seeing you today has filled me with joy, and most of all, such peace! I want you to remember that."

"Please do come and visit us in the city," I added, "Aleja would be so glad to see you. It would be just right for you to meet my children - your siblings - Alfonso and Consuelo. Not a day has gone by when I don't think of you - especially you - Hija. My prayers for you have been answered."

When I released her, she saw the tears in my eyes.

"Thank you", she said simply, in a voice choked with tears.

As she was about to go out the door, I called out to her.

"Fidelina, are you familiar with the name Fausto Bardilas?" I asked.

"Oh yes," she replied, "he works in a neighboring farm. I know him quite well."

"Fidelina, I may not have long to live in this earth. So, I might as well swallow my pride and tell you about Fausto. He is my son, Hija. He is your brother. I hope you will treat him as such from now on," I told her.

After talking to her, I just knew I could tell her anything and she would understand me and forgive me.

She did not seem surprised to hear about Fausto. She must have known it all along. She simply nodded her head and gave me that look which told me she understood.

Then, she went out the door and out of my life.

---

[63] *Sheer native shirt for men usually heavily embroidered, in Binisaya*

CHAPTER 26

FAUSTO

After the encounter with my father, I could not go back to the municipio to finish the documents. I simply went direct to the train station to take the train home, where I stayed very quiet for several days.

On the third day, I finally wept.

Then, I went to visit Fausto Bardilas at the neighboring farm.

"Fausto, do you know that you and I are siblings?" I asked him.

He did not seem surprised to hear this. He must known it all along. I told him about my encounter with our father.

"It happened when he was parish priest of Minglanilla," he calmly explained to me. "My mother's family was one of the tenants of the friar lands around Talisay. As administrator, Padre Antolin would have dealt with my mother's family closely."

"At that time, he must have been severely threatened by the impending rebellion. His very life would have been endangered," I reflected.

"He certainly needed a little mother then. Who wouldn't? Ah, Peding, we must think of him with compassion, if not love," Fausto said.

"Well, after all, you got those amazing brown eyes, Fausto," I teased him, "or are they green? Do they call you Señor Fausto, too?"

"No, Peding, because unlike you I am poor, and these brown eyes won't make me rich," he joked. He was not poor, having acquired ample land from his ancestor tenants-turned-owners, just like me. But, unlike me, he was too timid to speak out loud.

"You're a good man, Fausto," I assured him. "And you're my brother. I feel so fortunate. From now on, let's stay close to each other, won't we?"

"I think you have given me really wonderful news today, my sister," he answered. "I still can't believe my good fortune. I feel like a big thorn has been extracted from my insides - my father has finally admitted I am his son..."

And with that he broke down into sobs, shedding the copious tears which he had been trying to hold back.

"It matters not whether he has given me anything like money or property or even a name. The only thing I ask is that he recognizes me as his son..."

I went over and touched him on the shoulder.

"Oh, Fausto, I understand you only too well. I myself have been weeping in the past days since that encounter," I told him.

He covered his face with his hands, his shoulders heaving away.

"I have been waiting for this day...waiting..." he gulped.

"Fausto," I said after he had calmed down, "Loselo and I have bought some more farm land and we need somebody to take charge of it. Why don't you do the job?"

He readily agreed to my proposal. From that day on, Fausto and I worked closely together.

Then, I finally had another daughter whom I named Nicolasa.

DISCUSSION VII
The Reunion

"*Lola Peding and her father met when she was older,*" Susan, my cousin, liked to pass on this bit of folklore, "*she had been married and had several children at that time*".

"*Really? Tell me more about it,*" I prodded her.

"*She went to the municipio in Talisay to have some documents notarized. That's how she ended up in his office there,*" she said.

"*I thought he held office at the Ciudad near the Cathedral,*" I reminded her.

"*Yes, but apparently he also went to Naga and neighboring towns to do service there,*" she said, "*we all know transportation was not easy for many people at the time. So he came to them.*"

"*Anyway,*" she went on, "*there she was facing him across the table, with the documents between them. He read the names in the document, then he looked up and asked, 'so you are Nicolasa Bascon's daughter?'*"

"*Lola must have said yes, and he must have recognized her as his daughter,*" I said the obvious.

"*Well, I imagine he must have looked more closely at her face and noticed the hazel eyes. Then, he would have no doubt she was his daughter,*" she said. "*Actually, he said, 'you are my daughter'*"

"Gosh! Can you imagine your own father introducing himself to you at the age of thirty," I said, *"But, then such was life in those days. As you said, it was not easy to get around. That in itself would explain why people lost touch with each other."*

*"***Manoy Fausto Bardilas** *and Lola Peding would really have felt a thorn extracted out of them when their father finally acknowledged them himself,"* Susan mused, *"wouldn't you?"*

"And when Lola enumerated the names of her children, Lolo Frias remarked that she had named Tio Antolin Regner after him. So Lola told him that her next daughter would be named Nicolasa after her mother," Susan told me.

"That must have been before 1925 before Lolo Frias died, right?" I asked her and added, *"Anyway, Lolo Frias must have felt very proud to know Lola Peding. At that point, she and Lolo* **Loselo Regner** *were doing quite well, with him as official of the* **Philippine National Railway** *and the children all thriving and studying in good schools."*

"Lola Peding was a great disciplinarian. She had a very strong, assertive personality. It must have been the Latin temperament. She was also a survivor. Remember Lolo Selo died early and left her with ten children. And yet she managed all their landholdings with a strong hand and got her children through college," Susan declared.

"Oh, yes, that's right. But now back to Lola's encounter with her father," she added, *"Lolo Frias told Lola about Manoy Fausto Bardilas. He told Lola that Fausto was his son."*

"I have always wondered about that," I told her, *"and in fact I have been to see the church records at the parish church in Talisay. I found* **Fausto Bardilas'** *death certificate. He died in* **1977** *at the age of 85, so he must have been born in* **1891**. *At that time, Lolo Frias would have been the parish priest of* **Minglanilla**.*"*

"So **Maxima Bardilas, Manoy Fausto's mother** *was his little mother then,"* Susan said, *"although she lived in Talisay. Her family must have been one of the tenants of the friar lands. That's how the two would have met. That's the most likely explanation. Or she could have worked in*

the convento just like the Bascon sisters. What else did women do in those days?"

"Do you know that Maxima got married when Fausto was very young? Her husband's surname was **Empaces***," I told them. "It is just so amazing how all those women eventually moved on with their lives after bearing children out of wedlock, especially by a priest, which was really taboo and still is."*

"Ahhh..." everyone wondered for a moment.

"The 'survival rate' can be attributed to close family ties. The women and their families were self-sufficient farmers and they supported each other," I reflected. "People were less individualistic then."

"But, primarily, religious beliefs considered a child as a precious gift from God," Susan said, "no matter the circumstances surrounding its birth".

After a brief reflective silence, I said, "But we must not forget the women themselves. They must have been strong and resilient women. Lolo Antolin seems to have been drawn towards strong women, who were older. Now, I really think all he needed was a motherly hand."

"One can only make an educated guess. Anyway, Lola Peding and Manoy Fausto worked very closely from then on. In addition to Jose de la Cerna, she had just found another brother," Susan chipped in.

"What kind of person was Fausto?" the question came up.

"I was told by his grandchild, **Evelyn Amora***, that he was hardworking and very quiet. I told her that reminded me so much of my father, Sebastian. They were both of an introspective nature. I like to think they got it from their common ancestor, Antolin," I said.*

"And hear this!" I added, "Fausto's grandchildren through his daughter, **Nemesia Watin***, are all accomplished professionals. Worth mentioning is Evelyn Empaces Amora, a Math, Physics, and Chemistry professor. Another distinguished grandchild is* **Rev. Father Nestor Bardilas Watin***, a diocesan priest and a Canon lawyer. He obtained his degrees in Theology and Canon Law at the University of Sto. Tomas, just like Lolo Antolin. Inevitably, a great grandchild of Antolin Frias followed exactly in his footsteps as a priest and a lawyer."*

"How impressive! Where did you learn all this?"

"I met the Watins at a gathering in Talisay recently. The meeting was really quite unplanned. But I can feel the strong hand of Providence there," I replied. "Father Watin impressed me with his strong personality – really the perfect pastor, as he managed to talk to everyone in the room throughout the long evening. He exudes a powerful persona – a perfect mix of sharp mind and a soft heart. I just think Lolo Antolin lives again through him."

"By the way, you can google him. He is officially designated in New York, and he travels between the USA and Cebu at present," I added.

"He wants to meet all of us Frias descendants, including the ones in Naga."

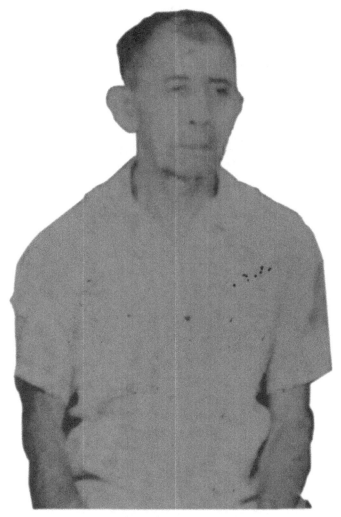

Fausto Bardilas, son of Maxima Bardilas and Antolin Frias (1891-1977)

Private Collection of the Author

CHAPTER 27

THE TRUTH SETS ME FREE

The Truth has always been elusive. It takes Wisdom to find it. Then, it takes Courage to face it. For Truth most often causes pain.

Truth is pushed aside for one's comfortable delusions.

Ultimately, Humility is needed to accept and live the Truth.

In my struggle for freedom, I broke my vows, strayed far from the truth to cater to my all too human needs.

But, I have loved, and loved deeply. But I have also caused pain to the people I loved.

Perhaps the descent into Hell is necessary on the road to Heaven. Perhaps the descent into the dead is necessary for one to rise again. Perhaps the soul has to go through St. John of the Cross's "dark night" in order to love the light.

So, now as I approach my sixties, I have been spending more time at the Church of San Agustin, helping my once fellow Agustinians in their sacred mission.

I and my family have come to terms with this. Although my renewed vocation has taken me away from home for long periods, my wife, Aleja, and our two grown children have encouraged my mission.

"Oh, Amor, I am so happy," Aleja told me again that day as she had been telling me every day. "Such peace! Thank you, Amor!" And she would hold me tight.

Having been loved and cherished by her affluent family all her life, she never really expected much more than the simple joys of each day. Yet, she always felt like she had received more blessings than she deserved. With our children grown and happily married, she has set me free to straighten up my life.

I have made peace with Fidelina and Fausto, and Fidelina would take care of Jose.

Having been both a priest and a lawyer has enabled me to help others – and what greater task was there than that of serving my fellowmen? My heart is overflowing with gratitude to God - for my life, for my wonderful family, my community, and for everyone my life has touched.

I won't be long now when I would find a still greater peace, more complete than any I have ever known. I can picture myself sitting for dinner with Aleja and suddenly turning pale. I would be clutching at my chest. Aleja would help me to our bed and call the doctor who would advise me to rest in bed for a week.

As I write this memoir now, I have been told of the suspicious flutter detected in my heart. Aleja, her heart heavy with dread, has been tending to me with unusual devotion, sitting up in our bed as I sleep, watching my every breath, and trying to cheer me up with funny stories when I am awake.

But I know God has other ideas, and one morning, I won't wake up. I will have died in my sleep.

I will finally go home.

Here, asleep in a silent grave/Rest in peace, without worldly pomp/ Neither gold nor marble nor even light powder/My name engraved//"

"Flowers of simple calyx/Buds of earth tell the passers/That someday there will born more beautiful/A virgin flower//"

"An Angel of Peace protects my grave/Where the faithful friend stands/Look, it says, pointing to heaven/That is your homeland//"

-ANTOLIN FRIAS, LA VIDA DEL CAMPO –

AN ANGEL STANDS ON GUARD OVER THE TOMB OF
ANTOLIN FRIAS AT THE CARRETA CEMETERY IN CEBU CITY

DISCUSSION VIII

"Antolin Frias, priest and lawyer, passed away in **September, 1925**. His remains lie at the **Carreta cemetery in Cebu City**," I read from my notes to the group before me.

"His grave is how he would have wished it to be as he expressed in his early poem, La Vida del Campo, in the lines, Silenciosa tumba, ni en oro or marmol *(a silent tomb without gold or marble nor even white powder)*. His remains are now in a bone chamber near the original grave which, according to the Suarez-Frias descendants, was nice. The specific spot in the Carreta, surrounded by centuries-old oak trees, is where distinguished Spaniards of those times are buried. And, as though his wish in his poem communicated itself generations after his death, the cemetery authorities placed a white statue of an angel over all the graves in this section of the cemetery", I added.

"He wrote that poem when he was in his early twenties" M. noted. "Doesn't that say something of him as a man – so young and already imagining how his grave would look?"

"Oh yes," I replied. "That too strikes me as very special."

"But does any of that really matter now? Things always seem to fall into place with the passage of time, and all that was chaotic eventually becomes whole. The events which caused so much pain and bloodshed *are then understood to be necessary — judging from its effects on the long term. So-so! Now, I am hungry. Let's go have some chocolate cake!!!" I suggested.*

"*So many unanswered questions are better left to the reader of my book on my great grandfather,* **Father Antolin Frias y Ramos, OSA.**"

THE END

Published Works Of
Fr. Antolin Frias y Ramos, OSA

MEMORIA sobre la influencia de la Iglesia en la civilizacion. Premiada con un crucifijo de plata en el certamen celebrado en Tortosa en 1881. (MEMORIA a recollection of the influence of the Church on the civilization. Awarded a silver crucifix in the contest held in Tortosa in 1881.)

A VIDA DEL CAMPO. Poesia publicada en al tomo II de la "Revista Agustiniana", p. 286. (Life in the Camp. A poem published in the "Revista Agustiniana", p. 286.

AL IlTMO Y RMO. Sr. D. Fr. Martin Garcia, dignisimo Obispo de esta diocesis a su llegada a Cebu. Himno, Ibiden, tomo XIII, pag. 368 (a hymn written to honor Sr. D. Fr. Martin Garcia, the dignified Bishop of Cebu.)

HIMNO, (the copy generously provided by Father Michael Co, OSA)

LA CONQUISTA DE CEBU, a one-act play written in Cebu and presented in 1890.

(https://groups.yahoo.com/neo/groups/circuloprogrisivo/conversations/topics/522)

Hymns and novenas, like the "**NOVENA**" to the Sto. Nino, which is referred to in the journal "*Anno* 1864 – Mision XCIII de Religiosos".

(https://book.google.com.ph/books?id)

Old issues of the *Revistas Agustiniana* would most certainly unearth more of his work.

THE DESCENDANTS OF
ANTOLIN FRIAS Y RAMOS

In his lifetime, Antolin Frias y Ramos acknowledged Fidelina Bascon Regner, Jose Bascon de la Cerna, and Fausto Bardilas as his children.

I. ANTOLIN FRIAS AND NICOLASA BASCON

A. Fidelina Bascon (1887-1954) married to Loselo D. Regner (railroad engineer)

1. Luis Bascon Regner (Civil Engineer-contractor; entrepreneur) married to Aniceta Chan
2. Antolin Bascon Regner (died early in the 1930's as a student) married to Amparo Cabantan
3. Elpidia Regner Arquillano (school principal) married to Isabelo Arquillano
4. Rafaela Regner Du (entrepreneur) married to Guillermo Du
5. Sebastian Bascon Regner (civil engineer and airline pilot) married to Trinidad Borromeo
6. Leo Bascon Regner (entrepreneur) married twice, first to Brigida Deiparine, then to Violeta Marine
7. Lorenzo Bascon Regner (civil engineer/ contractor) married to Praxedes Mancao

8. Andrea Regner Sta. Cruz (entrepreneur) married to Raymundo Sta. Cruz
9. Nicolasa Regner Lazo (pharmacist) married to Guillermo Lazo
10. Dionisio Bascon Regner (farmer/inventor) married to Paulina Bacus

II. ANTOLIN FRIAS and EUSTAQUIA BASCON married to APOLONIO DE LA CERNA

A. Jose de la Cerna married to Rosario Arañas

1. Isidra de la Cerna la Rosa
2. Juanita de la Cerna Mercado

III. ANTOLIN FRIAS and MAXIMA BARDILAS (1854 – 1957)

A. Fausto Bardilas (farmer) - 1892-1977 married to Eugenia Cabanilla

1. Ana Bardilas Bas
2. Quentin Bardilas
3. Nemesia Bardilas Watin
4. Angela Bardilas Brigondo
5. Primitiva Bardilas Empleo
6. Martin Bardilas
7. Genera Bardilas Seno
8. Alfonso Bardilas

The following names appear on official records as descendants of Antolin Frias and his wife, Aleja Suarez.

IV. ANTOLIN FRIAS and ALEJA SUAREZ

A. **Alfonso Suarez Frias – 1900-1963 (entrepreneur/landlord) married to Milagros Olmedo**

1. Fernando Olmedo Frias (businessman) married to Rosario Aranas
2. Antolin Olmedo Frias (businessman) married to Marina Teves
3. Vicente Olmedo Frias (executive Judge; CPA; government auditor)) married to Clarissa Saguin
4. Ruben Olmedo Frias (businessman) married to Adelaida Miranda, then to Heidi Frias
5. Alfonso Olmedo Frias, Jr. (businessman)
6. Rogelio Olmedo Frias (business executive) married to Leonor Guaniza

B. **Consuelo Frias Zacarias married to Vicente Zacarias (prominent lawyer)**

1. Noli Frias Zacarias
2. Salvador Frias Zacarias
3. Avelina Frias Zacarias
4. Nenita Frias Zacarias (a lawyer)
5. Carmeling Frias Zacarias (a nun)

THE END

REFERENCES

Books:

Bernad, Miguel B. (1972), The Christianization of the Philippines. Manila: The Filipiniana Book Guild.

Blair, Emma Helen, (1903). The Religious Estates in the Philippines. The Philippine Islands. Cleveland, Ohio: The A.H. Clark Company.

Gowing, Peter G., ThD (1967), Islands Under the Cross. The Story of the Church in the Philippines. Manila: National Council of Churches in the Philippines.

Labrador, Paulino B. (1992), Historical Study on the Emergence of Urban Settlements in the Province of Cebu, 1565-1898. Cebu City: University of San Carlos thesis.

Pilapil, Vicente R., (1962), Nineteenth-Century Philippines and the Friar Problem. Washington, D.C.: Academy of American Franciscan History, Vol XVIII No.2.

Sales, Todd Lucero (2008), Argao: 400 Years in Legend and History. Municipality of Argao, Cebu.

Vano, Manolo O., PhD (2002), Christianity, Folk, Religion, and Revolution. Quezon City: Giraffe Books.

Mission C V de Religiosos, Augustinian publication

Internet:

Argao, Cebu. Retrieved from https://www.google/com-ph/webhp? sourceid=chrome-instant & ion

Burrell, David (1991) A Historian Looks at Hegel Philosophically. Critical Examination of Hegelian Dialectic, Determination, and Contingency. Retrieved from www.historical.com

Castrogeriz. Retrieved from https://en.wikipedia.org/wiki/Castrogeriz

Cebu Lifestyles. Retrieved from Cebu Lifestyles.com/articles/ Cebuano-art-and-culture.

https://en.wikipedia.org/wiki/Burgos

en.wikipedia.org/wiki/Order of St. Augustine.org

(**https://www.google.com.ph/GR** No. 10397.US v. Go Seng.31Phil. **204-Philippinelaw.info**)

(**https.chanrobles.com/scdecisions/jurisprudence 1924/dec 1924/ gr 1-22399 1924.php**)

www.mocavo.com/Journal-of-the-Philippine-Commission-4/ 500711/814

www.mocavo.com/Journal-of-the-Philippine-Commission-4/ 500711/814

(en.wikipedia.org/wiki/Taft_Commission)

(https://www.google.com/webhp?sourceid=chrome-instant& ion=1&espv=2&ie=UTF-8Hq=valladolid%20spain

THE AUTHOR SPEAKS

When I was born in Cebu City, Philippines, in 1947, the Second World War had just ended, leaving my country struggling to get on its feet.

So the Cebu of my early years was pervaded by a strong American presence, especially in business and education. Remnants of 300 years of Spanish colonization persisted, especially in religious beliefs and the strict religious upbringing in Catholic schools. We eventually established our own unique culture, a blend of different cultural influences which touched our shores.

Thus was my character and that of the Filipino people shaped – an interesting blend of east and west.

I studied at the University of San Carlos, the Colegio de la Inmaculada Concepcion, and St. Theresa's College, all Catholic institutions in Cebu City.

My 20-year career as marketing staff of Philippine Airlines enabled me to travel extensively throughout the USA and Europe. Later, I had a second career as a college teacher of English at several Cebu City universities.

In 2007, I immigrated to the United States to join my grown children, where I traveled back and forth for seven years. There I worked as an Adjunct Instructor of English at Ocean County College, New Jersey, for three years.

My husband, Franklin and I, have seven wonderful children – Anna, Lorenzo, Patricia, John David, Josemaria, Miriam, and Enrico.

The rich, varied culture surrounding my life, added to frequent world travel, has captured my interest in History and the Humanities. This strong interest finally led me to write this first book, a historical novel based on the life of my great grandfather, a controversial Spanish friar of the nineteenth-century Philippines.

From the vantage view of time I have seen how the Hand of God has worked behind all world events. What has seemed unforgivable in our History has suddenly appeared indispensable and necessary. Ultimately, the missing pieces of a puzzle are always found, and a beautiful harmonious picture emerges from a chaotic mess.

I presently reside at 18 Acacia St., Lahug, Cebu City, Philippines.

EVELYN REGNER SENO, **Author**

Printed in the United States
By Bookmasters